LUCILLA

a novella

PARALLEL UNIVERSE PUBLICATIONS

BOOKS BY DAVID A. RILEY

NOVELS

The Return
Goblin Mire
Moloch's Children
Into the Dark (as Andrew Jennings)

COLLECTIONS

The Lurkers in the Abyss & Other Tales of Terror
His Own Mad Demons
Their Cramped Dark World and Other Tales
After Nightfall & Other Weird Tales
A Grim God's Revenge: Dark Tales of Fantasy & Horror
A Handful of Zombies: Tales of the Restless Dead

ANTHOLOGIES

Things That Go Bump in the Night (with Douglas Draa)
Classic Weird Volumes 1 & 2
Kitchen Sink Gothic Volumes 1 & 2 (with Linden Riley)
Swords & Sorceries: Tales of Heroic Fantasy Volumes 1-7
(with Jim Pitts)

LUCILLA

a novella

David A. Riley

Clouds hung over the rooftops like soiled linen, stretched endlessly across the sky.

In sheer desperation, she flew fast beneath them, her body ragged from all the wounds to it, but feeling triumphant. The crows that had attacked her had long since tumbled to the ground, dead, some dismembered by her claws. Though she knew she wouldn't be able to last much longer. Her falcon's body and its inadequately tiny avian brain couldn't cope with her presence. She would need something larger, or she would die - completely this time.

Downwards in a long, parabolic swoop, she soared towards the rooftops. Somewhere down there she needed to find a refuge.

Something with a brain large enough to accommodate her but not too mature its host would resist her invasion.

Then she saw her.

1

"Make sure the front door's locked, will you?" Mary Milligan paused halfway up the stairs; her arms hooked under four boxes of A4 paper. "One of Alice's neighbours rang to say her husband has found out where she is. He's threatened to force his way in."

"Is he drunk?" Miranda asked as she turned the dead lock before securing the safety chain behind the heavy door. She glanced through the fisheye lens, but the lamplit street looked deserted. Only parked cars, one of them hers. She remembered Alice's face when she arrived at the Women's Shelter a week ago, fresh from hospital. Bruises on her round, childlike face had left a patchwork of purples, browns, and jaundiced yellows. Despite telling herself that it was ridiculous, that she should be able to deal with issues like this, Miranda felt an instinctive dread of the brute who punched his wife so viciously only the intervention of the police saved her life. After three years of working at the Women's Shelter, she knew she should have become inured to things like this, but she hadn't, thankfully perhaps. Unlike Mary, who had run the shelter for over a decade and seemed able to take everything in her stride.

"Drunk?" Mary emitted a brittle, artificial laugh, edged with sarcasm. "Men like that use drink as an excuse when they have to face up to what they've done in court. Believe me it doesn't take getting drunk for the likes of the Karl Browns of this world to turn his fists against his wife."

Miranda said nothing. Mary loved to lecture, seemingly indifferent to how many times she may have trotted out the same tirades. After working with her for as long as she had, Miranda had heard them all.

She glanced at her watch. It was nearly six; almost time to be going. It had been an exhausting day and she was ready for a few hours' relaxation and the mug of hot chocolate she would eventually have before bed.

That or the half bottle of Chardonnay left in the fridge.

All she had left to do now was finish some paperwork, then she could go.

As she stepped into the office at the back of the building, she jumped as the telephone rang only inches from her. Thoughts of Karl Brown had certainly begun to affect her nerves, she thought, though in all fairness to herself, she remembered, it was only a few months since an earlier husband managed to barge into the house armed with a baseball bat, which he swung on anyone he saw inside the building while screeching to be taken to "that bitch of a wife". Miranda had taken a blow to the head when she tried to disarm him before four other women managed to hold him down till the police arrived, summoned by the panic alarm that Mary had had the presence of mind to trigger. Miranda still suffered occasional migraine attacks from the blow. Sometimes, for all that the refuge had security doors, she felt so bloody vulnerable here.

Though she was careful not to let this become obvious to anyone else, especially the women sheltered here. That would have been unforgivable.

Steadying her nerves, Miranda reached for the phone.

"Hi, it's Claire at Social Services."

Miranda recognised Claire Simpson's voice straight away – simultaneously realising that any thoughts of getting away in the next few minutes had probably gone.

"What can we do for you, Claire?"

"I'm sorry to ring so late. It's a bit of an emergency."

Wasn't it always?

"A young woman's been passed on to us by Social Services at Preston. We need to fix her up with somewhere to stay for the night. If you have the room, that is."

"We're nearly full but we might be able to squeeze one more in at a push. We could put an extra bed in one of the larger rooms."

"That would be fantastic. I know it's a nuisance, but these things hardly ever happen at convenient times, do they?"

"Is it bad?"

"Pretty bad, Miranda. The police are looking for the man now. Seemingly he threatened to kill her."

The way Claire said "seemingly" struck an odd chord with Miranda.

"Are there doubts about his threats?"

Claire sighed. "Maybe. She has been hurt. That's true enough. She turned up at A and E with cuts to her arms that needed stitches." Claire hesitated for a moment. "The thing is no one really knows who she is or where she lives. She's confused – or won't tell us anymore. All she'll say is that whoever attacked her will kill her if he finds where she is."

"Sounds like she could do with police protection rather than boarding in a place like this. We're not equipped to deal with threats like that, not if they're serious."

"That's just the point. No one's sure just how serious they are. For all we know she might have hurt herself."

"In which case I'm not sure she should come here at all. You know we don't accept people at risk of self-harm."

At that moment Miranda heard her boss reach the bottom of the stairs and called out to her. Passing her the gist of the message, she handed Mary the phone, hoping she would agree with her reluctance. To her surprise, though, Mary said: "Bring her round. We'll find room for her somewhere. No probs, Claire."

As Mary replaced the phone on its cradle, Miranda said, "Are you sure we should be taking her in? Isn't she a risk?"

"What would you have me do, Miranda? Ship her off to a psychiatric ward because social services aren't sure what really happened? Or put her out on the street? Really, Miranda, I thought you had more compassion than that." Mary impatiently brushed her fingers through the greying, short-cropped hair above her ears. "We'd better get ready for her. She'll be here soon enough. Room four will do. There's only Olivia and Glenda in there and there's more than enough space for a third bed. I'll speak to them while I get some sheets if you'll root out the spare bedstead."

With that she hurried upstairs, leaving Miranda with the realisation that any thoughts of getting away within the next half hour had gone. Not that she would have minded normally but she felt exhausted today. Since the attack last month, she still found it difficult to sleep – at least without several glasses of wine to dull her thoughts. A year ago this would have seemed unthinkable but bit by bit she had begun to feel affected by the tales of violence from the women here. Like Chinese water torture, it had begun to wear her down, and she knew she might sometime soon have to think about a change of career.

Academic theories were all very well, but the harsh reality of male violence was something she found impossible to deal with, resonating as it did with memories of how her father had behaved to her mother. The callous shit had been the epitome of professional respectability to anyone outside their family unit, chairman of the local golf club, a prominent member of the Chamber of Commerce as well as being a leading town councillor and one-time mayor. Unlike some of the brutes she had heard of here he had never provided evidence of what he did. If he hit her mother it was always to the abdomen or hard enough to hurt but not bruise, though twice when Miranda was away at university her mother had "slipped" and broken her arm. It seemed a Godsend when he succumbed to sclerosis of the liver, dying after months of invalidism a broken, bitter wreck of a man.

Miranda pressed two fingers to the bridge of her nose, pinching it hard. She had to stop dwelling on old memories. All they did was depress her. And she knew she was prone to that already.

With the help of two residents Miranda managed to manhandle the spare bedstead up the stairs to where Mary had cleared space in room four, a large, square-shaped room at the front of the house, its bay overlooking the street, along which most of the other premises housed solicitors, accountants or semi-governmental agencies.

They had barely finished putting everything in place when the doorbell rang.

"Sorry it took so long," Claire said when Miranda answered it moments later, still breathing hard from rushing downstairs. "Traffic was horrendous." A thin, waif-like girl stood beside her, a professionally fastened bandage covering most of the lower part of one arm where she had been stabbed. "This is Lucilla."

Rarely had Miranda seen anyone less substantial than the girl. Was she a size zero like one of those anorexic horrors of whom she sometimes saw photographs in magazines? Though there was nothing bony or malnutritioned about the girl's face, Miranda thought, strangely enough. Perhaps it was the girl's pallor, which after what she was alleged to have gone through was understandable, though everything about her looked colourless too, from the pale blond hair that hung to her shoulders, to her light beige coat and bleached jeans, as if she had deliberately tried to make herself as bland as possible. Stood next to Claire, who was almost six feet tall, most women looked short. Lucilla looked more like a worried child pretending to be a woman, and Miranda supposed she was probably less than five feet tall, perhaps no more than four eight or nine.

"Lucilla." Miranda offered the girl her hand. Surprisingly, when the girl responded, her fingers felt like a bundle of dead leaves beneath her own. And, though she resisted the temptation, Miranda felt an irrational urge to wipe her hand down the side of her skirt afterwards.

Mary Milligan strode towards them from the staircase. "Lucilla-with-no-last-name, I believe," she boomed. Mary's gaze managed to be benevolent, stern, and understanding at one and the same time. And a bit of an act, Miranda thought, hoping she was not being uncharitable. "Perhaps you will remember what your last name is when you've been with us a while?" Her smile broadened.

Lucilla nodded. Just.

"She's very tired," Claire told them. She held a carrycase in one hand, which she passed to Miranda.

"Just a bundle of clothes, that's all, I'm afraid. Not even a credit card." Though Miranda wondered if the girl was even old enough to have one. And, though she knew that girls could get involved with violent, abusive men at any age, she wondered how much truth there was in the girl's story. Now was not the time to ask. She assumed Social Services had done their bit to verify what she had told them, and if Claire Simpson was satisfied that would have to do for now. Besides, Miranda knew it was up to Mary to decide on matters like this. It was silly of Miranda to worry when Lucilla would probably be gone by the time she came in to work tomorrow, like so many others.

Even so, when she finally drove home to the quiet solitude of her one-bedroom flat, Miranda could not help thinking about the girl. She had such a sorrowful, wistful face it felt even more wrong than usual to see it touched by fear. Although Lucilla said little, and what she did came in such quiet tones that Miranda struggled to hear what she said, she could not help being impressed by the girl's sincerity. Something bad had happened to her, Miranda was sure. Nor did she doubt Lucilla's fear of being found by whoever it was who was looking for her. If only the girl would tell them her surname – or at least the name of the man – then the police might stand a chance of finding him. As it was, on what little they had to go on, Miranda doubted if much of an effort would be made.

That night Miranda dreamed about her father for the first time in years. A tall, thin-featured, sarcastic man, with broad shoulders and an arrogant beak of a nose which, thankfully, she had not inherited, he had had a way of talking down to her as if he knew even before she opened her mouth that what she had to say was of no importance to him – which was probably true, she thought, even when she passed her exams and was accepted to university. Only one person's views had validity in their household so far as her father was concerned, and those were his own.

In her dream he was still as he had always been till the sickness set in. Her mother was there too, slumped on the sofa, doubled-up. Punched once more, Miranda knew, which was when her dream self-found a baseball bat – the same, she was sure, that was used against her at the shelter last month. Angrily, she raised it into the air, but the more she struggled to swing it down against her father's head the more sluggish she became, till she found she could barely move. Frustrated, she shouted at him, but even her words wouldn't come. His smile grew contemptuous as he stared at her…

When she awoke it was still an hour before dawn, but she could not sleep anymore. Her heart was pounding, and she was covered in sweat as if she had been running. She felt sick at the memories of the man she had grown to hate so much she found it difficult even now, after all these years, to regard other men without suspicion. Miranda climbed out of bed and padded, stiff-legged with sleep, into the kitchen where she made herself a mug of coffee before going into the living room. She turned on the TV for the early morning news, as much to pass the time as from any interest in what was being broadcast. Several mugs of coffee later and she dressed for work, feeling leaden and depressed. And wishing there were some way she could burn all those memories of her father from her mind.

2

During the next few days Lucilla settled into the shelter. Though she refused to leave the building even to the small back garden with its potted plants and plastic seats for some fresh air, she was in every other way no problem, tidying up after herself and doing as much as she could to help the smooth running of the place, though Miranda wondered if many of the others even realised she was there most of the time, she was so unobtrusive.

Miranda could not help liking her, though even after a few days she felt that she still did not know her any better than the night they first met. Not that she may have wanted to do. Dreams about her father continued to disturb Miranda's sleep and she felt as if her own psychological problems were enough for her to worry about. Other than that they were already shorthanded at work, with one staff member on maternity leave and another on long-term sick, she would have asked for time off, but this time of year they were always busy. Perhaps it was the build up to Christmas and the financial worries that burdened families more than any other time that saw so many break down in violence. Whatever the cause, she knew she would have to stay on and 'man the fort', as Mary would put it with all the *joie de vivre* of a Girl Guide leader.

Despite her worries, Miranda was fascinated how

well Lucilla seemed to get on with the handful of children staying at the shelter. Meg Tattersall's daughters were three and five years old respectively. Kylie, the older of the two, a freckle-faced girl with ginger hair, took to Lucilla in particular and was rarely away from her side. In the hot-house atmosphere of the shelter, though, it didn't take long for this to cause friction with her mother, who already had problems over doubts about her own self-worth. Despite medication from her doctor, Meg's jealousy quickly grew out of all proportion at the burgeoning friendship. Only Mary's timely intervention prevented this from spilling over into violence, although Lucilla seemed unable to understand what had caused it. Miranda wondered if the girl was a complete innocent, impressed by how she had somehow managed to hold onto an almost breathtakingly childlike naivety after all she was supposed to have been through. Though bruises and even broken bones were common amongst most of the women at the shelter, stabbings like the one that Lucilla had suffered were rare, if only because these almost always led to custodial sentences for those responsible. As, no doubt, would happen to whoever attacked Lucilla when he was finally apprehended and charged with what he'd done. Despite the severity of her wound and the bruises that had now begun to fade, Lucilla seemed unaffected by them, outwardly at least.

"How are things today?" Miranda asked a week after Lucilla's arrival at the shelter. She glanced at the wound on the girl's arm. Lucilla had finally removed the bandage that previously covered it and Miranda could for the first time see the full extent of what had been done. She was surprised how long and savage it looked. Starting from just above her elbow, it extended downwards to within an inch of her wrist, a long, disjointed, jagged line, at one point splitting into two, held together by rows of stitches. Though starting to heal, the edges of the wound were brick-red and still looked sore. To Miranda it looked less like a knife wound than as if something much blunter had been gouged through her flesh.

Puzzled as she was by the wound it was only after several seconds Miranda realised that Lucilla was watching her intently.

"It's much better now," the girl said, her voice soft. "It's stopped hurting. I took the bandage off so the air could heal it."

Which was the most Miranda had heard the girl say in one breath since she arrived at the shelter.

"That's good," Miranda said, unsure if she had made a mistake in letting the girl see her interest in the wound. "It must have hurt like hell."

Lucilla shrugged silently, and it was obvious to Miranda she was unwilling to talk much more about it.

When she was alone in the office with her boss a few hours later, Miranda took the opportunity to ask if Mary had seen Lucilla's wound.

"Is it healing all right?" Mary barely looked up from what she was reading, pen at the ready.

"Apparently."

"That's good."

"Have you seen it?"

Laying down her pen with a sigh, Mary said, "What's the matter, Miranda?"

"Lucilla's wound. Claire told us she'd been stabbed. I've seen enough knife wounds to know this isn't one."

"It was what Claire told us when she brought her here. I assume she was informed by someone at the hospital or by the police. Surely they would know?"

"Can we be sure someone else told her? It may have been Lucilla."

"And if she did, why would she lie?"

Miranda shook her head. "I don't know. I wish I did. If you looked at the wound, though, you'd agree."

"If it wasn't caused by a knife, what do you think did it?"

"An animal, a claw maybe... I don't know." Even to her she sounded unsure of herself and was hardly surprised when Mary laughed.

Exasperated at her boss's reaction, Miranda said, "Take a look at it first, then laugh." Embarrassed suddenly at her inability to express herself more clearly, Miranda stood up and left.

Less than an hour later, Mary called her into the office.

"I've taken a look."

"And you agree with me?"

"Maybe. I'm not sure."

Mary picked up the phone, speed dialling Social Services.

"Claire, is that you?"

Miranda took a seat opposite, listening.

A few minutes later, Mary replaced the phone. "Claire can't remember who told her."

"*Can't* remember?"

Mary shrugged. "From what she said – which isn't like Claire at all – all she could tell me was that she 'vaguely' remembers hearing about the girl being stabbed but can't remember who it was who told her."

"Couldn't she phone the hospital for confirmation?"

Mary stared at Miranda with a look of infinite patience. "Aren't we in danger of making too much of all this? The wound is healing. In a few days' time, the way she's responding to being here, I'm sure Lucilla will feel like telling us more herself."

"She still hasn't told us who she is." Which was something both of them had talked about already. "That needs resolving."

"In time, Miranda. There's no need to rush."

Unsure why she felt there was more wrong with Lucilla than Mary seemed able to appreciate, Miranda reluctantly let it drop. She knew her boss well enough to realise when she had pushed her as far as she would go. Besides there were other, more urgent matters for her to attend to, not least finding somewhere for Alice Brown to move now that her husband had discovered where she was. There had been no urgency earlier in the week while he was being held in police custody after attacking one of his neighbours who had tried to persuade him not to find his wife. Now he was about to be released on bail. It was only twenty miles from where he lived to the shelter.

Alice was already in the communal kitchen, her few possessions bundled in carrier bags around her feet as she waited for transportation to a shelter in Blackburn. She had been here three weeks and had started to forge strong friendships with most of the older women. Miranda tried to comfort her, but the distress Alice felt was obvious.

"He might not come," she tried to insist. "He knows the police will arrest him again if he does."

"We can't risk it," Miranda told her. "It's the rules. You can't stay in a shelter once your whereabouts are known. You must move to another. It's for your own safety. Everyone else's too."

Alice nodded as tears spilled down her hollowed, prematurely aged cheeks. She'd had a hard life, moving from one council house or flat to another, half the time her husband in prison or living with other women. But like the bad penny he was, he always returned when times were hard, and he needed her. And, though Alice understood why she had to leave, that didn't make it any easier for her to accept. This was probably the first place she had felt safe for years, surrounded by women who shared her problems.

Miranda glanced at her watch. Nicola had volunteered to drive Alice in her car and had gone to collect it. Miranda wondered whether it would have been better if she had said she would take her instead. Her Fiesta was parked only yards away. How long had it taken Nicola to get back here? She hoped the girl hadn't taken the opportunity to do a bit of shopping, though Miranda would hardly have been surprised if she had. It didn't take twenty minutes to walk to the multi-storey in town and drive back here.

A group of women had already gathered in the hallway to give Alice a hug and wish her well when she left. Miranda noticed Lucilla amongst them, almost hidden beside the taller women, a waif-like figure, so tiny she looked more like one of their children than a resident herself. Miranda wondered how long the girl had been involved with the man who attacked her. Where were her family? Surely, she must have a mother somewhere. Sisters perhaps? A father? But so far Lucilla had mentioned none of them to Miranda. Nor had she said anything about her family to anyone else, so far as Miranda knew – which was strange. Once they had settled in, women at the shelter were usually only too willing to talk about themselves, to unburden their problems with others who had gone through the same brutalising mill. Not Lucilla-with-no-last-name. She remained a closed book to everyone.

Miranda heard a key in the front door. At last, Miranda thought to herself, though it had taken Nicola long enough to return. Miranda reached for Alice's bags when the door burst open and Nicola, a startled look on her face, fell into the hallway, a man behind her. He was rough, unshaven, with stained sports pants and a hoodie top. Pushing Nicola ahead of him with the flat of a large, tattooed hand, he gave her an extra hard push at the last second that sent her sprawling into the gathered women.

"Where the fuckin' hell is she?"

Miranda knew at once who he was. She didn't even need to see the white-faced look of terror on Alice's face to realise this.

Karl Brown staggered forwards, belligerently drunk, his breath rank with stale beer.

"Where the fuckin' hell is the two-faced bitch?"

Miranda saw her boss stood in the doorway to the office. She knew Mary would have already pressed the panic alarm. In a few minutes the police would be here. In the meantime, all they needed to do was minimise what harm the man could do. At least he did not appear to be armed. After the baseball attack earlier this year, Miranda had a dread of something like that happening again. Clenched fists were bad enough, but it would take years for her to forget the pain of that day, when she was left concussed on the floor, a hairline fracture to the side of her head.

Brown lurched forwards. One of the women tried to hold him back but he cuffed her from him with a backwards swipe of one hand that knocked her off her feet.

In a few strides he would reach his wife. Miranda knew she would have to intervene to stop him. God alone knew what he could do if he was allowed to attack Alice. But fear held Miranda back. What happened last time was still too vivid. She could still feel the ache down the side of her temple.

Another of the women stepped in front of the man. Amazingly even tiny, fragile Lucilla stood there too. At the last second, though, the first woman lost her nerve, shuffling back to leave Lucilla to face the man by herself. At which point Karl Brown reached down and grabbed the girl's shoulder. Miranda tried to move forwards. The man towered above the girl, and Miranda knew he could easily hurt her. His thick fingers, daubed with crude tattoos, buried her shoulder as he tightened his grip. Lucilla swayed under the weight of his fist. Her own hands stretched towards him as if she thought she could hold him back with them.

Don't, Miranda thought. You'll anger him even more if you do. You'll make him hurt you.

Make him *want* to hurt you.

Karl Brown didn't hurt her, though. A puzzled, worried, confused look on his face, he stared down at her. His hand dropped from her shoulder. At the same time a bead of blood appeared in a corner of his mouth. He licked it back, but another bulged from between his lips, larger this time, drooling down the side of his chin – which was when Karl's wife started to scream. The man's face had become pale, a dirty, clay-like pallor bleaching his skin beneath the stubble.

A police siren howled outside the Shelter. Miranda caught sight of the flashing lights of the police car through the open door as two constables burst into the hallway, flinging themselves on Karl Brown. While they pinioned his arms to his sides, a third policeman read him his rights. Whether from the alcohol he'd drunk before coming here or from shock at being arrested, Karl slumped between them. His legs buckled as they dragged him out onto the street, before starting to heave him into the back seat of their car.

It was over within seconds, so fast Miranda was barely able take it in, though she was aware of Alice sobbing somewhere behind her and of Mary telling everyone to calm down in her usual stentorian voice, telling them that everything was all right. Nicola sat nursing her knees at the foot of the stairs, obviously enjoying the concern of those around her. Feeling detached somehow from all of this, Miranda searched for Lucilla. She tried to see past the women crowded about the hallway, despite Mary's efforts to usher them into the dining room where there was more space, but she could not see her.

"Where's Lucilla?" Miranda turned to the nearest woman.

"Lucilla?" Several teeth missing from years of drug-abuse, Joyce Grainger's face looked even more dumbfounded than usual. "Lucilla who, dear?"

Impatiently, Miranda brushed past her. "Lucilla," she shouted, though she was unsure why she felt an overwhelming concern that something was wrong.

She ran up the stairs, though she had not seen Lucilla head this way. Instinct? A premonition?

Whatever it was that prompted her, Miranda went straight into the room that Lucilla shared with Olivia and Glenda. Despite her uncertainty, she was not surprised to find Lucilla stood by the bedroom window, staring down at the street. The police were still there. While one of them was talking on his radio, the others were leant inside their car as if they were suddenly concerned about their prisoner.

"Are you all right?" Miranda asked.

Startled, Lucilla turned to face her, a look of guilt on her small face.

Did she think she'd somehow harmed the man?

"Good grief, what's the matter?" Miranda asked. "Whatever happened, it wasn't your fault. Nicola should have been more careful when she came in. She should have seen him waiting on the street and realised that something was wrong. It was inexcusable." As she would soon make clear to Mary when she saw her, Miranda thought.

Lucilla shook her head.

"I didn't mean to hurt him."

"Hurt him? You?" For an instant Miranda was tempted to laugh, but she knew that would have been the wrong response. Lucilla needed better confirmation of her innocence than that. "He'll be all right. He was probably shocked the police arrived so quickly, that's all."

Though she knew Karl Brown had begun to look ill even before the police burst in. There might have been only seconds in it but, unless the man had second sight, he could not have known he would be bundled away within the next few minutes. She remembered the drops of blood on his mouth. Had he suffered a seizure, brought on by rage, alcohol and clogged, unhealthy arteries and a lifestyle that would probably see him dead in the next few years?

She glanced through the window. The policemen had dragged Karl out of the car and laid flat him on the pavement. One was knelt over him, pumping his chest with both hands. Despite her concerns over Lucilla, Miranda moved nearer the window, the girl beside her.

In the distance another siren was heading their way, hidden beyond the grey rooftops.

After minutes of strenuous effort, the policeman finally stopped pumping the man's chest and slumped forwards. Miranda drew Lucilla away from the window and back into the room.

"Is he dead?"

Miranda shook her head. "I don't know," she lied.

Downstairs she heard the doorbell ring and knew one of the policemen must have returned to the Shelter. Even up here she could hear Alice's hysteria, and wondered how a woman who had been beaten and betrayed by a man like Karl Brown should care so much when he died. When her own father passed away years ago Miranda had felt nothing inside her, only a sense of relief that he would no longer be there to scorn or belittle her or furtively hurt and humiliate her mother. Yet to hear Alice's sobs she would have thought the woman had lost the love of her life.

"It wasn't your fault," Miranda told Lucilla as they headed for the stairs.

With the sudden death of her husband, the whole reason for Alice having to stay at a Shelter had gone. During the next few hours Mary busied herself cancelling arrangements for her transfer to Blackburn, while trying her best to help console the woman. It was quickly agreed that Alice could stay on at the Shelter overnight before they helped her back to her home.

It was a bad business. Mary was quietly concerned about security at the Shelter and was determined to make sure its locality was kept as much out of the news as possible. It was the first time anything like this had happened and it created a strained atmosphere amongst everyone, not helped by some furtive glances cast towards Lucilla.

Kept busy for the rest of the day, Miranda was not able to see as much of Lucilla as she would have liked. She was unhappy at how the girl had been affected by what had happened and the certainty Lucilla seemed to have that she was responsible in some way for the man's death, absurd though Miranda knew this was. Others, though, were not so sceptical, and Miranda was aware of whisperings amongst some of the women.

"I'm not sure if it would be a good idea for Lucilla to stay much longer," Mary told her when things had settled enough for them to relax for a few minutes over a pot of tea. Sat in the office, they had as much privacy here as anywhere in the Shelter.

Both had noticed how the other women, even some of the children had begun to shy away from the girl, though no one would say why.

"It's absurd in this day and age that people could suspect someone as small and frail as Lucilla to be responsible for that man's death." Miranda felt her cheeks burn with indignation, though she normally tried to preserve an air of professional detachment when talking to Mary.

"Of course, it is," Mary said. "But we are not dealing with educated, rational people, Miranda. Much though I regret having to say it, most of them are barely literate. And some have had what common-sense they ever had battered out of them. This is what we have to face, like it or not."

"Which means what?" Miranda asked. "Send Lucilla elsewhere?"

"That would be the logical solution. We can't afford more trouble. Not until what happened today has been forgotten."

"But what did happen?" Miranda said. "A man burst in, drunk to the gills, and died. It was probably a stroke or a heart attack or something like that. If it hadn't happened here, it would have happened somewhere else. He was a walking time bomb."

"You may suspect that's what happened. If it matters, so do I," Mary said, so reasonably that Miranda felt irritation well inside her. "It's what the rest of them think. I've seen them looking at Lucilla-no-last-name. They're frightened."

"What did they see that we didn't?" Miranda asked. "Sparks burst from Lucilla's fingers?"

Mary started to laugh at the absurdity when there was a knock at the door.

It was Joyce. Her hand hovered across her mouth where her teeth were missing.

"I thought you might want to know. There's trouble in the kitchen."

Miranda followed as Mary rushed from the office towards the communal kitchen at the back of the house. It was a large, rectangular, comfortable room where many of the women liked to relax over endless brews of tea. When Miranda walked in, she sensed a change. There was tension in the air, and she knew straight away the cause. Lucilla was stood in one corner. Most of the women, including the two she shared a room with, were facing the girl, their hostility obvious.

"Is something the matter?" Mary asked, reasserting her authority. "You know we don't stand for trouble of any sort in the Shelter. That's not why you came here." She cast the bulk of the women a scathing glance. "At least I hope not," she added.

Miranda saw they had probably arrived just in time before something serious happened. Just words, she thought, though it was obvious no one wanted to step forward to explain what had been going on. She looked at Lucilla. "Would you like to come with me for a while?" Lucilla nodded, moving quickly to her. As they left the room, Miranda could sense a collective fission of relief behind them, though no one spoke other than Mary as she lectured them on the importance of getting on with each other.

Miranda took Lucilla straight to the office.

"Sit down," she said. "Would you like some tea?"

Lucilla declined a drink, though she sat down quietly, looking even more childlike than usual. Miranda noticed the cut on her arm looked healthier now and was healing well.

"What happened back there?"

Lucilla looked up, and Miranda noticed how intensely pale the girl's eyes were, with only the slightest hint of green. She seemed unable or unwilling, though, to explain anything.

Miranda might have pressed for an answer, but Mary returned a few moments later, still fuming over what had happened.

"Those damned silly women. You'd think they'd learn from their own experiences, wouldn't you?"

"Does anyone?" Miranda felt tempted to ask but stayed silent.

Mary looked down at Lucilla.

"What shall we do with you?" She turned to Miranda. "They won't have her with them. Olivia and Glenda. They won't tell me why, of course, but they're adamant they don't want her in their room."

"Must we send her to another shelter?" Miranda asked.

At which Mary turned to Lucilla once more and said, "I'm sorry, my dear, but that's what it looks like we'll have to do. I don't know what you've done to upset them all…"

Miranda looked at her watch. "It's too late now. We can't ship her miles away at this time."

"Though I'm loath to leave her here overnight," Mary said.

Miranda's suggestion came almost as much as a surprise to her as it did to Mary. "She can stay with me," she replied almost before she had thought about it. "We can sort out where she goes tomorrow." She shook her head at Mary as her boss was about to say something. "I know it's unorthodox. And perhaps we shouldn't do things this way. But I feel we're responsible for what happened this morning. If Nicola hadn't been so careless when she came back, Karl Brown would never have had the chance to burst in and perhaps none of this would have happened."

"You still don't need to do this," Mary said, though not as insistently as Miranda had expected.

Miranda glanced at Lucilla. "I think I do. Besides, I've plenty of room. I've a bed settee I'm sure is immense enough to accommodate someone as big as Lucilla. And I could do with the company."

"For one night only," Mary added. "No more. Tomorrow we make arrangements for another Shelter to take her in."

At six Miranda waited while Lucilla put together what few possessions she had, then led her out to her car. It was the first time the girl had left the building since she arrived, and she was obviously nervousness when she stepped outside. Her small hand tightened about Miranda's, reinforcing the impression she was only a child. A child with the figure of a full-grown woman, Miranda thought.

During the drive across town Lucilla remained silent, sitting next to Miranda so still it was almost as if she had frozen solid. Whenever Miranda glanced at her the girl's eyes were focussed straight ahead as if she feared looking to either side – or was perhaps so frightened she dared not move.

By the time they arrived at the estate a mist had started to spread across its flat, open plan lawns, softening the outlines of the red brick flats, built in units of four, two up, two down. Miranda's was on the first floor, accessed by a flight of stairs behind an outside door. After parking in her reserved space nearby, Miranda wasted no time in taking Lucilla indoors. There was a nip in the air and the girl wore only a light linen coat hardly thick enough for weather like this.

She led her into the living room and switched on the TV.

"I'll make something to drink," she said. "I'm sure you're ready for a cup of tea to warm you up."

She left the girl watching a repeat of *Friends* while she went into the kitchen, wondering how long the evening was going to seem if the girl remained as silent as she so far had.

"You've never spoken about the man who attacked you," Miranda said sometime later after they had finished a microwaved lasagne from the freezer. Though she had not intended to take the opportunity to probe into the girl's background, something about Lucilla's reticence prodded her into it. Besides, tomorrow morning the girl would be gone. The more information she could pass on to the next Shelter the girl went to the better able they might be to cope with her. Or so she told herself. Though in truth she knew curiosity about the girl's background had more to do with it. She was puzzled why the rest of the women at the Shelter had taken against her. Did they suspect her of stealing from some of them? That was the usual cause, though she had heard no whispers about it. And in a place as tight knit as the Shelter, she knew she would have been aware somehow.

"I don't like to talk about him," Lucilla said finally.

"Sometimes it's good to talk about things," Miranda said. "Helps put them into some sort of perspective. It can help other people help you too."

Lucilla looked at her, doubt in her face. There was something about her body language that made it clear she was not going to say any more about it.

You are a strange little girl, Miranda thought, discarding her curiosity as much as she could, though frustrated by it.

By ten o'clock Lucilla had begun to doze. At which point Miranda decided she might as well have an early night. She went for some sheets and a duvet and set about converting the sofa into a bed. By the time she had finished, Lucilla tumbled into it more asleep than awake. With a shake of her head, Miranda wandered into the kitchen, decided to leave the unwashed plates till tomorrow, and reached for a bottle of wine. This and the book she was reading would help get her a good night's sleep.

By twelve o'clock, half a bottle and several chapters later, Miranda tiredly switched off the light and rolled over. Before she hardly knew it, she was drifting into a deep, dreamless, satisfying sleep. It was the kind of sleep she would normally have only woken from when her alarm went off at seven in the morning.

Long before then a scream jolted her up in bed, her pulse racing.

Remembering the girl, she knew straight away who it was.

A nightmare, that's all. That's what must have made her scream, she thought.

Miranda switched on the light and reached automatically for her mobile as she rolled out of bed, before running across the room to the door.

The sparsely furnished living room was gloomy when she stepped inside. Apart from the light in the bedroom behind her, the only illumination came from the afterglow of the streetlamps outside, refracted across the curtains. A silhouette of Lucilla – or a Lucilla-like figure – was stood at the window.

Miranda reached for the light switch.

And saw Lucilla curled up on the bed-settee, her hands clinging to the duvet she had pulled around herself as she stared wild-eyed at the curtains.

Miranda quickly followed her gaze. Her heart still pounding, she strode to the curtains and pulled them open, but there was nothing there.

Though disturbed at what she thought she had seen, Miranda was relieved to find they were alone. Crossing to the girl she cradled her head. It felt light within her arms.

"Bad dreams?" she asked, though she did not expect a clear answer. She wondered if Lucilla was prone to nightmares, if that explained why the women who shared a room with her at the Shelter had turned against her. Who would want their sleep broken at three in the morning by screams like this night after night, especially when they were recovering from domestic violence themselves?

"Do you often wake up like this?" Miranda asked.

Lucilla nodded her head.

"Every night?"

Again, Lucilla nodded; she looked up at her.

Miranda was unsure even when it happened what motivated her as she leaned forward, stared into Lucilla's pale green, almost translucent eyes, and kissed her, gently at first, but with increasing, devastating urgency, on the lips. It was as if something compelled her, something stronger than anything she had known before. In her mind's eye she could see Lucilla's face, but it was different, radiant, part angel, part devil, greater than anything she had ever known, against which she felt what will she had melting like snow before an opened furnace.

And it was that image of an opened furnace, its flames roaring with a terrible rage, that lingered on…

3

"Disappeared? How?" Mary's face was a picture of abject shock. "She was in your charge, Miranda. How could you let her walk out and leave without you knowing?"

Miranda shuffled, uncomfortably aware how incompetent she sounded. "She must have got up and dressed while I was asleep and let herself out. It wouldn't have been difficult. It was something I never expected to happen, though. How could I?"

Mary sighed. "I knew I should never have agreed to let you take her home. It was most unorthodox. Nothing good could come of it, I knew."

"She could have left the Shelter any time she chose," Miranda pointed out. "She wasn't our prisoner."

"Thank you, Miranda, for reminding me of that."

"I'm sorry. I didn't mean to offend you."

"You haven't. Though I am disappointed. There are bound to be consequences. There are all those threats she reported to the police."

"Which don't seem to have been taken all that seriously. Has anyone contacted us about them since she arrived at the Shelter?"

Mary admitted no one had. "So far," she added, sighing again, in resignation this time. "I suppose what's done is done and there's nothing we can do about it. Though I do not look forward to all the questions I'll have to face when word gets out that I allowed you to take her home last night. I don't know what I was thinking of in agreeing. I really don't."

But Miranda knew they would easily weather whatever storm they faced, especially since she was sure it would in reality be no more than a squall, and a small one at that. Though what the consequences would be if anyone discovered the girl had not gone missing, but was still in her flat…

Which was when Miranda wondered what came over her. She had never done anything like that before, not even in her dreams. It was as if she had been taken over by an overwhelming urge, unbidden, unexpected, shocking her more than it did Lucilla, who responded to the intimacy with so much passion she wondered, when she thought about it now, if the girl had egged her on.

Had enticed her, perhaps?

Though there was nothing she could remember Lucilla doing she could pinpoint as encouragement.

All she knew, as she exited Mary's office, was a warm aura of self-contentment at the thought of Lucilla waiting for her when she returned back home.

She had not, till now, suspected just how lonely she was.

Or how lonely she would be if Lucilla left – which was a thought that suddenly made her feel queasy inside.

Don't be stupid, she told herself, alarmed that she should be panicking so soon about things like this.

Was this the kind of vulnerability she had trapped herself in?

To prevent herself from dwelling on the possibility that Lucilla might have gone by the time she returned home, Miranda spent as much of the day as she could with work, so that by six o'clock she was more than ready to head for her car, when all the hopes, doubts, happiness and fears she had managed to push to one side before returned with a vengeance.

Concentrating on driving through town helped to quell most of them till she drew up outside her flat, when they surfaced again, almost making her sick.

What was wrong with her? She had never felt like this before. If this was what love was like, she wondered if it wasn't something she would have been happier without.

As she locked her car and all but ran to her flat her heart felt leaden yet light at the same time. Inside, as she mounted the stairs, she became aware she could smell cooking – and almost wept at the realisation that Lucilla was waiting for her, a meal prepared for her return.

The girl stood in the living room, a smile on her face as Miranda strode in, knowing her own lips betrayed a bigger smile.

4

Over the next few days Miranda was aware of a few knowing looks on the faces of many of the residents at the Shelter. She knew she had changed. Even Mary remarked on it once with what may have been something of an air of suspicion – which warned Miranda to temper her feelings whenever the two of them were together. Mary was no fool. It would not take long for her to work things out if she gave her enough evidence. She needed her job at the Shelter and could not afford to put it at risk. Even so, by late afternoon she was impatient to be on her way. Only sheer exhaustion had ever made her feel like this before, when what she longed for then was the chance of a good night's sleep.

"Have you found yourself a nice feller?" one of the women at the Shelter asked. For all that the woman had only ever had abuse from her spouse, Maggie Wainwright had somehow managed to maintain an indefatigable faith in love, fuelled perhaps by all the drivelly romantic novels she seemed to read.

"Why would I do that?" Miranda asked, suppressing a smile. "Don't you think I hear enough from you lot to warn me off men for good?"

"They're not all bad," Maggie said. "Mine is. Don't I friggin' well know it? Not everyone is as unlucky as me, though. Some can tell the good from the bad. Wish I could. Would have saved me a few hard knocks."

Trying to avoid giving away too much, Miranda briskly got on with her work, aware that gossip quickly spread through the Shelter, most of it ending sooner or later in Mary's ear.

She wondered how long she could keep Lucilla a secret.

She was not normally a secretive person and she would have liked nothing better than to tell everyone what had happened. But she knew Mary would take it bad, especially after Miranda had told her the girl had gone missing. She could already hear Mary's lecture on how important trust was at the Shelter. Probably just seconds before she told her to hand in her notice.

But her returns home at night made it all worthwhile.

After the first few days she could barely remember what life was like before Lucilla lived with her.

She still knew virtually nothing about the girl's past. Lucilla was not a great talker, and about herself she was even quieter than about anything else. Miranda still knew nothing about the man who had threatened to kill her, who had beaten her up and gouged her arm. Perhaps that was for the good. She did not really want to know anything about him, so long as he never discovered where she was.

"Would you like to go away for a holiday?" Miranda asked on their third evening together. "Although we're a bit short staffed at the Shelter, I'm sure I could wangle a week off – or a long weekend at least."

"Don't you like it here?" Lucilla asked.

"Of course, I like it here. Wouldn't it be nice if we could spend some time together, get to know each other? I miss you when I'm at work all day. A few days away would do us good."

But she could tell Lucilla was unenthusiastic about leaving the flat. Miranda remembered how reluctant the girl had been to step outside the Shelter, as if the outside world frightened her. Perhaps Lucilla had psychological issues, like agoraphobia. She knew illnesses like that were more common than most people thought.

"Or we could stay here, enjoying each other's company," Miranda added, which immediately seemed to cheer the girl up.

Lucilla's nightly bouts of terror continued, though she managed to restrain them by clinging tight onto Miranda whenever she woke up in the early hours of the morning, her body soaked in perspiration. She would not talk about what caused them, though Miranda knew they were dreams of some sort. If she were awake Miranda could tell when they were about to happen. The girl's body would start to writhe about the bed as if she were struggling to run. There was an electrical quality to the air about her when this happened, which sometimes woke Miranda up long before they reached their climax.

Other than Lucilla's unsettled sleep, though, little marred their stay together. Lucilla was an amazing cook, if sometimes bizarre – and Miranda wondered whether most of what she had learned about cooking had been from someone who had spent a lot of time abroad or been born overseas. Not that she was inclined to grumble. Anything was better than the one-person ready meals she lived off before, microwaved from the freezer.

Despite her optimism that she could persuade Mary to let her have a few days off, her boss was far from pleased when she asked.

"You know we're short staffed," Mary said. "Christmas looms – which is always a hectic time for us. Brings out the worst in some men."

"Just a couple of days?"

Mary shook her head. "Really, Miranda, I'm surprised at you for asking. I thought you were a committed team member." She peered at her from over her reading glasses. "Is there a special reason you want time off?" she asked.

Miranda felt herself colour up. "I just feel I need a break, that's all. I'm overtired."

"Aren't we all," Mary said, matter-of-factly, though her eyes remained trained on hers. Miranda felt as if she was being scrutinised. "You've changed," Mary said. "I don't know how, but you're different."

Miranda frowned. "I feel the same to me," she lied, perhaps more defensively than she had intended. "Perhaps more tired than I was. The stress of this place. Other than that…"

Mary sat back and glanced at the duty roster in her desk diary. "If you really feel you need time off," she said finally with undisguised reluctance, "perhaps I could let you take a couple of days. Though I really shouldn't. Till Anne-Marie and Jennie return we really are desperate for staff."

5

Miranda was overjoyed when she arrived home that night.

"Mary's let me take two days off next week. Along with my weekend roster that means we can have four full days together."

Lucilla smiled doubtfully. "We aren't going away?"

"Not if you don't want to, silly." Miranda gave her a hug. "When you feel up to it, we will. Till then, I don't mind slobbing about here."

That night Lucilla's nightmare seemed worse than usual. Not since that first time had Miranda heard her cry out like this.

"What is it?" Miranda whispered, holding onto the girl's shoulders as she shook beneath her, her breath coming in high-pitched, almost asthmatic wheezes.

The bedroom felt cold and Miranda's first thought was that something must have gone wrong with the central heating as she sat up shivering in bed. Outside, something large flitted across the window, before passing out of sight, like a massive owl, silhouetted in the gloom. Lucilla moaned. She opened her eyes and clung to her, distracting her from whatever she glimpsed.

"Don't let him get me."

"No one's going to get you," Miranda said,

wondering how bad the girl's experiences with her attacker had been – how long she had known him. If only Lucilla would open up about what had happened, she knew she would have a chance of helping her.

The next day, though, Lucilla seemed to have recovered from her nightmare and Miranda was able to set off for work with a clear mind, pleased at the girl's resilience.

"I have a meeting to attend later this morning," her boss told her when she arrived at the Shelter. "You'll have to hold the fort while I'm out." As Deputy Manager this was something Miranda had done numerous times already. Not that there were often any problems to deal with. For the most part life at the Shelter was so humdrum it was almost boring, which was as it was intended to be, a sanctuary within which women whose lives had been broken by violence could find time in which to heal.

"No probs," Miranda said as Mary collected her briefcase and coat. "When do you expect to be back?"

"By lunchtime." She smiled briefly as she bustled to the door.

After this, a minor squabble between several of the residents took up the next half hour before Miranda could start to deal with other matters. Having fallen behind by this stage, it was a matter of getting her head down to catch up when her mobile rang.

Glancing at it, she saw it was Lucilla, ringing from the flat.

"What is it?" she asked.

"You must come home straight away."

"Why? What's happened? Has he found you?"

"Please come back, Miranda. I need you here."

There was such intense desperation in the girl's voice Miranda said, "I'm on my way." She glanced at her watch. It was nearly eleven, an hour at least before Mary was expected back at the Shelter. Besides Miranda there was only Nicola in the building, who she knew she shouldn't leave by herself. Barely seventeen, Nicola had only worked at the Shelter for a few months after leaving school. But what could she do? She knew Mary would go ballistic if she came back and found she had left Nicola in charge, but Miranda couldn't ignore the fear in Lucilla's voice, whatever happened.

For her part Nicola looked pleased at being asked to look after things, as if this was a possible short cut to promotion. Let her keep her illusions, Miranda thought, too preoccupied with worrying about what was going on at her flat to be bothered about that. Outside, her car started straight away, and it was only a short while before she was roaring down the short stretch of tarmac towards her flat. Pulling up abruptly, she abandoned her car and ran towards the flat, her door key already clasped in her fingers.

"Lucilla, it's me," she called out as she rushed up the stairs. The door at the top was already open. Lucilla was stood beside it, tears glistening down her cheeks.

"I couldn't help it," the girl blubbered.

Miranda saw the body lying face down on the

living room carpet.

"My God, Lucilla, what have you done?" Miranda recognised Mary's clothes at once. Her leather briefcase lay on the carpet beside her. Pushing it to one side, Miranda knelt to move Mary's head so that she could see her face. She flinched when she saw the woman's features. Drawn in a grimace, her lips were no more than a bloodless slit curled back so far from her teeth that her gums were bare. Hesitating for a moment, Miranda touched her boss's face with the tips of her fingers, feeling the hard rigidity of the muscles that had locked across it in a final, paralysing spasm.

"When did this happen?" Miranda asked, though she knew Mary only left the Shelter a couple of hours ago. It didn't seem possible for her body to have become so cold and stiff so soon.

"She was banging on the door," Lucilla said between gasps, wiping tears from her eyes with the back of her hand. "She knew I was here. She was calling my name. She wouldn't leave."

"You let her in?" Feeling shaky, Miranda stood as she wiped her hands down the sides of her pants.

"I had to, Miranda. She said she'd ring the police."

That was Mary all right. All bluster and threats if she had to be. How was the girl to know they'd be no more than that? That Mary would have given up eventually if Lucilla had only kept her head and stayed out of sight? There was no way Mary could have known for certain that Lucilla was here.

"What happened?"

"She stormed up the stairs. She said you had betrayed her."

"And then? How did she end up like this?"

Lucilla shook her head, sobbing. "I don't know, Miranda. She had a heart attack, I think. She was so angry, so red in the face. She kept shouting at me – till the pain hit her."

Miranda looked at Mary's face. The pain-wracked, frightened expression frozen across it could have been caused by a heart attack. But would that explain how her body had become rigid as if rigour mortis had already set in?

"Did you ring me as soon as it happened?" Miranda asked.

When Lucilla nodded, Miranda knew that Mary could not have been dead much more than thirty minutes. Even from what little she knew about it, she was sure she shouldn't have been stiff like this yet.

Feeling sick, Miranda went into the kitchen. She poured water into the electric kettle, though she was sorely tempted to drink something stronger than the tea she was about to brew.

"What do we do now?" Lucilla asked behind her.

Miranda shook her head. "I don't know," she said, struggling to take it in, finding it hard to grasp what had happened, and wondering if somehow, in some way Lucilla had killed Mary.

As she added milk to their mugs of tea, Miranda looked at the girl. Her face was blotchy and red, tear stains shining down her cheeks. She looked distraught and frightened. And Miranda wished she could go up to her and clasp her in her arms, soothing her, but she couldn't, not now. Not with Mary's body only yards away in the living room.

Miranda knew that whatever they were going to do, they would have to make a decision within the next few minutes.

If only she could be certain Mary died from a heart attack. But she remembered what happened to Karl Brown. He died from a heart attack too.

Why hadn't Lucilla phoned for an ambulance when Mary collapsed? Surely, she hadn't died straight away. Mary had looked as fit as a flea this morning. It was hard to believe she could have dropped down dead in the middle of shouting at Lucilla.

What alternative was there, though? That Lucilla had been responsible? That she had been responsible for what happened to Karl Brown too? She knew that was ridiculous.

Miranda sipped at her tea, feeling the warm sweetness calming her nerves.

"What do we do now?" Lucilla asked.

"We think. Think hard," Miranda said, which was what she had already started to do. At least there was now no need to rush back to the Shelter. Only Mary would have made an issue of her absence, though she dreaded to think what might be happening with Nicola in charge. Hopefully, the girl would have the sense to ring on her mobile if she needed help. Till that happened she had time in which to try and sort out this mess. Which was what? Phone for an ambulance? But how would she explain Mary being in her flat? And why no one had phoned till nearly an hour had passed since her attack? No self-respecting doctor would look at the body and not ask why she had been left so long. They might even suspect she had been dead longer. Even to Miranda it was hard to believe that Mary died so recently.

Questions, questions, questions.

There would be multitudes of the bloody things.

And most would be from her superiors, putting her position at the Shelter at risk, not to mention any hopes she might have of promotion.

Especially if word leaked out about Lucilla.

She glanced at the girl, who was calmer now as she sat on an arm of the sofa, drinking her tea, looking smaller than ever.

What could they do about Mary?

What *should* they do about Mary?

The longer they waited the worse it would look if she were discovered here. Already they had probably left it too long, Miranda thought. Which was when she decided they would have to remove her from the flat.

Miranda remembered seeing Mary's VW Polo parked outside in one of the spaces left for visitors, not realising at the time whose it was. Putting aside her tea, Miranda returned to the living room. She steeled herself and knelt once more beside Mary, feeling in the pockets of her coat. Seconds later her fingers came across the thick bunch of keys she had seen so often in the past, usually tossed onto Mary's desk.

She told Lucilla what she was going to do.

"I'll need your help to get her downstairs. I'll fetch her car as near as I can to the foot of the stairs. If we're quick, we can carry her body out and get her inside the car before anyone sees what we're doing. It's usually quiet around here during the day, with everyone at work, so we have a good chance of getting away with it."

"What are you going to do with her?" Lucilla asked.

"Drive her somewhere else so it will look as if she started to feel ill, parked up and died." Her voice sounded cold-blooded and unusually calm, which was more than she felt. "I don't want anything to connect her with my flat."

Miranda knew this was risky. It escalated things further than she would have liked, but she dared not risk letting anyone know her boss died here. Too many questions would be asked, for which she had no answers.

By one o'clock she had driven Mary's car to an empty stretch of land near a derelict factory. Few people used it and it was quiet. No shops, no houses, no workplaces open. And she did not expect anyone to see her when she left the car to walk back to her flat over a mile away. Far enough not to make anyone jump to any conclusions there might be any connections between them. Annoyingly, Lucilla was unable to help. She asked if Lucilla could drive her

Fiesta to the site with her, but the girl said she couldn't drive, though Miranda was far from sure if this was not just an excuse to avoid stepping outside the flat. Even helping her lug Mary's body to the Polo seemed to take every scrap of resolve the girl could muster, fleeing back inside the flat as soon as they had finished.

Miranda felt exhausted by the time she arrived at the Shelter.

"I was starting to panic," Nicola said as if announcing something of monumental importance as soon as Miranda stepped inside the building. "The police have been on the phone." The girl looked flustered but pleased with herself.

"What do they want?" Miranda asked, shedding her coat as she strode into the office, feeling the onset of panic – and trying to conceal it from Nicola.

"They wouldn't say. They wanted to speak to you or Mary."

Miranda felt sick as she sat at the desk and stared at the phone. Had someone seen what she'd done and reported her to the police? Already?

"Thank you," she said. She nodded at the door, dismissing the girl, which earned her a scowl as Nicola turned on her heel and left. That she might have upset her didn't bother Miranda. She needed solitude in which to collect her thoughts before she rang the police. She looked at the note Nicola had scribbled on a post-it gummed to the computer monitor. "*Detective Sergeant Harridan – tel: 24165.*"

Miranda took a deep breath to calm her nerves

then punched out the numbers on the phone.

"Sergeant Harridan." The man's voice sounded bored, as if he'd had too many calls already.

"Miranda Walters. You left a message for me to ring you."

He thanked her for getting back to him. "I wanted to ask about one of the women at the Shelter. I don't have a last name," he said. "I don't know why, but all we know is she's called Lucilla."

Miranda glanced at the open doorway, relieved to see no one there. She stood up and carefully closed the door, though that was something Mary Milligan would have rebuked her for. Not now, she thought. Not anymore. Her open-door policy had died with her, for the time being at least.

"She's no longer here," Miranda said. "She left days ago."

"Damn it." The policeman seemed to collect himself and apologised. "Sorry about that, but we've had some developments."

"Can I help?"

"Only if you can tell me where she is."

Miranda hesitated. "I might be able to find out," she said. "I'm not sure if I can, but I could try. If it's important…"

"It is. Any help you could give would be useful."

"She's not in trouble, is she?"

"Would it matter if she was?"

Miranda laughed dismissively. "If she's done something wrong, I wouldn't protect her, if that's what you mean. It's not our job to hinder the police. We depend on you too much, especially when it comes to protecting our residents."

Sergeant Harridan sounded mollified when he replied. "I forgot. I should have realised that." He seemed to think about what he was going to say next. "Something odd has happened."

And for a moment Miranda felt a recurrence of her nervousness. "Odd?"

"The girl claimed to have been attacked. We checked the address she gave. No one seems to be there. As we didn't have a search warrant, that seemed to be it. A few days later some of our men had to visit the premises again. There'd been complaints from neighbours about a bad smell. Someone from the council called there and claimed to recognise what it was. He'd had experience at cleaning out places in the past where someone had died and not been found for weeks."

"Someone was dead?"

"You'll read about it soon enough in the papers, so I'm not giving anything away. Four bodies were found in the house. First reports are they died from natural causes. Heart attacks."

"Four of them?"

"Exactly." The policeman's voice was blunt. Disbelieving. "Too much of a coincidence, I know. We're still awaiting detailed results from the post-mortems to see what they really died of. Till then we're looking on their deaths as suspicious. One of them was holding a length of wood. There was a nail at one end caked in blood as if it had been used in a fight."

Miranda visualised the jagged cut down Lucilla's arm. Which had looked as if something like a claw had gouged it. Or a nail, she thought, feeling sick.

"You think Lucilla might know something about these deaths?"

"Perhaps," the policeman said, non-committal. "It's a long shot. But she's all we have at the moment."

Miranda wondered if they had checked the blood type to see if what they found on the nail coincided with the girl's. If they hadn't, they would, she was sure of that.

"I'll see if I can find something out for you, Sergeant. I'll ring you back if I do," Miranda said, eager to end the conversation as soon as she could.

"Would you ring even if you don't, Miss Walters? I'd like to meet you to discuss the girl."

"Of course. Certainly."

With a mumbled good-bye she slammed down the phone. No sooner had she done so than she reached for the plastic waste bin under the desk and was violently sick, retching into it again and again till her throat felt raw. It was minutes before she finally finished, wiped her mouth with a handkerchief and stared across the room, barely focusing on the white painted wall opposite, with its charts and graphs. She pictured Karl Brown lying stretched on the pavement outside the Shelter as a policeman tried to save his life. And Mary Milligan curled on the floor in her flat, a ghastly expression of pain transfixed on her face.

Now four more deaths.

All heart attacks.

Maybe, she thought. *Maybe*.

Miranda closed her eyes. How could someone as small and fragile as Lucilla be involved with this? It made no sense.

It made no sense at all.

She knew, even before it happened, that the day could only worsen. Too tense to eat, she skipped lunch, and stayed at her desk unable to work, staring at nothing. And waiting. Waiting for the call that eventually came at three o'clock that afternoon.

It was a policewoman this time. They had found the Shelter's telephone number in Mary Milligan's briefcase, though one of the policemen who discovered her body recognised her from a recent visit to the Shelter.

"What would you like me to do?" Miranda asked, trying to steady her voice.

"Do you know her next of kin? We need to contact them."

Miranda gave her the number of Mary's sister. Although Mary had once been married, she had been divorced for more than ten years and would not have thanked anyone for contacting her ex.

To Miranda's relief that was it. Nothing more was required. For now, she thought, certain that when Detective Sergeant Harridan heard about Mary's death, he would be puzzled at one more heart attack.

She finished early, too impatient to return home. She knew she would have to have it out with Lucilla tonight, one way or another. Though she dreaded it too. And her drive across town took all her concentration. It was getting dark early, and the streets looked gloomy, dispiriting. There was a light rain, and what little she could see could do nothing to ease her feelings of dread.

Shivering, she hurried across the puddle-strewn tarmac towards her flat as soon as she'd parked up, clutching her coat against the wind.

Lucilla was sat on the sofa looking listless when she pushed the door open into the living room. The lights were off, and the room was lit only by the television screen. Lucilla muted the sound with the remote control.

"Is something wrong?" the girl asked as Miranda stood in the open doorway.

Which was when Miranda's resolution failed her.

She shook her head.

"Nothing we can't cope with," she said. She peeled off her coat and hung it behind the door. "I need a hot drink." Though what she really needed, she knew, was a *strong* drink.

She went into the kitchen, unwilling to talk to Lucilla yet. She felt torn between the need to find out what had happened and fear of destroying whatever they had between them.

It was not till much later, after they had eaten and washed up afterwards, then settled in the living room on the sofa, a bottle of wine on the coffee table, that Miranda told the girl about her telephone calls.

"Will they question you more?"

Miranda took a long sip of her wine before saying, "I think so, Lucilla. It depends on whether the inquest finds that what's suspected of having been heart attacks really were."

"Why do you say that? What else could they be?"

Miranda felt like saying, "You tell me," but couldn't. She again sipped her wine instead. She could feel Lucilla's eyes watching her. Intent. Probing. She felt uncomfortable under their pale green gaze. Even alcohol was doing little to dull her feelings of guilt tonight. She had known Mary Milligan for years. It was Mary who interviewed and took her on at the Shelter. And, though she had often disagreed with her over the years, she had admired and liked her, and they had developed a friendship of sorts. A friendship she would miss. She could hardly believe Mary died in this room only hours ago. Nor did she think she would ever forget the look on Mary's pain-wracked face. She closed her eyes and the image became clearer, sharper, filling her with a feeling of disbelief. She wished she knew what really happened when Mary confronted Lucilla here. She remembered when the girl barred Karl Brown's way into the Shelter, how she raised one hand towards his chest. How he stopped, before falling back from her. How the police blundered in, snatching hold of the man before dragging him out into the street where he died.

Miranda opened her eyes. Lucilla was staring at her, concerned.

Worried.

Worried about what? That Miranda might doubt what really happened?

"The police were asking about you," Miranda said, though she really did not want to talk about it. "They've been back to the house where you were attacked." She paused and wondered whether the girl's face now looked tense. Or was that her imagination, wishing it on her? "They've found bodies."

"Bodies?"

Miranda involuntarily narrowed her eyes for a sharper view of Lucilla's face. Was her innocence feigned? Was it real? She yearned to be sure that Lucilla had nothing to do with this. Like Sergeant Harridan, though, she had concerns over too many heart attacks.

"They're carrying out autopsies to find out how they died."

She felt cruel telling her this, as if she was somehow trying to force Lucilla to react. Perhaps she was. The girl's lack of response was worrying, as if she did not care.

"What do you think they will find?" Lucilla asked.

"Heart attacks, I suppose. What else could they?"

That night Miranda fell asleep as soon as she climbed into bed, her head swimming from two bottles of wine, which were more than she would have normally had, but she'd felt she needed them tonight. Lucilla said little all evening, as if absorbed with too many thoughts of her own.

Sometime between two and three in the morning, Miranda's dreams were interrupted by a loud noise. Struggling to regain consciousness, Miranda's impressions of what was happening were jumbled together with her dreams and she had difficulty piercing through them to reality.

She sat up in bed, her head pounding from a hangover. She was aware of a violent banging. Something hard, like fists, were being beaten against the door downstairs. Loud. Intense. Lucilla's screams became shrill. And, despite the pounding in her head, Miranda piled out of bed, staggered towards the window. She glimpsed what could have been a face outside, before she realised there was no one there. No ladder rested against the sill, and the narrow patch of lawn below was empty too.

Shaken by her hallucination, Miranda returned to Lucilla and gripped her shoulders, her fingers gentle but firm, though they trembled with fear.

"There's nothing," she told her. "There's nothing to be frightened of."

Lucilla's eyes stared back at her. For several moments she was motionless, then she reached out, touched Miranda's sternum between her breasts. Immediately she felt the breath within her lungs shrink to nothingness and she was gasping for air. She whistled sharply as she sucked it into her mouth, but it was as if it disappeared into a terrifying void. Terrified at what was happening to her, she flung herself back from Lucilla, breaking away from her tensed fingers; immediately she could feel her lungs fill up with air and she could breathe once more, though her heart was pounding harder than ever.

Lucilla climbed across the bed towards her, but Miranda pushed herself back across the carpet till she collided with the back of the chair at her dressing table. Scrambling, she took hold of the chair. She swung it in front of her, the ends of its legs aimed at the girl.

"Get back," she warned. She was panting for breath and her arms ached with the effort of supporting the chair in mid-air.

Lucilla paused. "I'm sorry, Miranda. I didn't mean to."

"Like fuck you didn't. Is that what happened to all the rest?" Though she felt bewildered at what had happened – and why – she was sure that Lucilla caused it. She felt frightened too, as if she had found herself alone with a dangerous animal. "How did you do it? Some kind of martial arts trick?" Though who would teach something as deadly as that?

Again, there was a noise at the downstairs door. This time there was no mistaking it. Miranda did not know whether to look towards the sound or keep her eyes fixed on the girl.

There was an even louder series of thumps against the door. In that instant, Lucilla raised her eyes to the lamp hung in the centre of the ceiling. She reached for something on the floor – it could have been an empty wine glass – and flung it upwards. The bulb shattered.

Panic-stricken, Miranda scrambled towards the bedroom door. Her hand reached for the handle and pulled at it with all her strength. Before she could get out, Lucilla grabbed her shoulders and with unexpected strength flung her back into the room. Before Miranda could do anything, the girl fled outside and the door slammed shut behind her. Hearing someone burst into the living room, Miranda grasped the door handle with all her strength to stop anyone from opening it from the other side. The veins on her neck rose with the effort. No one – no *thing* – was going to enter the bedroom while she had any strength left in her arms.

She closed her eyes, wishing she could dam her ears to the sounds that came from the other side of the door. The screams; the floor-shaking bangs and crashes; the splintering of wood as furniture was hurled across it; the rending of cloth being ripped apart – *or what sounded like cloth* – all the while her head pounded with an intolerable ache that threatened to burst. White lights flashed before her eyes, though her eyelids were shut in concentration as she held as tight as she could to the door handle with aching hands. Then she could see Lucilla's face staring at her, though her eyelids were shut. She could hear her speaking to her as if deep inside her head. Simultaneously there came a terrible pain as if her skull was about to split open.

She knew she passed out. During that time it seemed as if hours had passed by, with time frozen, though when Miranda came to she knew it could only have been minutes before other sounds cut through her consciousness. Sirens were wailing, their stridency dying seconds later as footsteps clattered up the stairs. The door into the bedroom was pushed open as policemen in protective jackets spilled into it. Someone took hold of Miranda's arms. They prised her fingers from the bedroom door. She tried to resist, but three policemen were holding her now and there was nothing she could do to stop them from pulling her back across the room.

After that she was surrounded by confusion. She saw a policewoman's face, a mixture of horror and disgust on her thin features. Handcuffs were secured with what seemed unnecessary roughness about her wrists as someone started to read her rights, the man's voice thick with revulsion.

It was all so unreal. All the wine she had drunk didn't help, of course, especially when she threw up inside the patrol car as it took her away, a blanket draped about her head. She tried to tell the policemen in front what had happened, but they weren't listening to what she said. Nor did she get any more attention at the police station, where she was locked in a cell with a metal bed, a couple of blankets and a stainless-steel toilet, in which she again vomited, her body wracked by convulsions. Before they took her from her flat Miranda had glimpsed what they found in the living room – and knew that they blamed it all on her. But she hadn't – she *couldn't* have done that to the girl.

She closed her eyes, her head still aching, shivering though the cell was warm. She huddled beneath the blankets as she remembered the blood and debris, the shadows that flitted about the walls and ceiling as if something deranged had been let loose inside the room as the curtains billowed inwards from the shattered window, the torches of the police, and the glimpsed horrors of what had been Lucilla.

Miranda was left till morning, probably, she supposed, to give their forensic experts time to study evidence at the flat. She was given breakfast, though all she could manage was the mug of coffee. Her head hurt even worse than before and she felt sick, though most of the wine she'd drunk had been purged from her system, leaving its aftertaste – and that of the vomit – clinging to her mouth and down her throat.

Wretched, she sat on the edge of the bed till they came for her.

Did she want a solicitor?

"What for?" she asked.

She was told it was her right to have someone advise her, but she didn't want anything, she told them, just the truth.

She was led to an interrogation room by a policewoman. Sergeant Harridan and a plainclothes detective entered seconds later. The other man was older than Harridan, with a careworn face too thin to be healthy. His eyes regarded Miranda with deep interest. Harridan unfastened a brand-new cassette, placed it in a tape deck on the table and switched it on. He gave the time, his name and rank and that of his colleague, Detective Inspector Phillip Butler.

"Do you remember what happened?" he asked. There was a cautious hint of a smile on his lips as if he wanted to show he was still unsure of her guilt.

"I'd been drinking," Miranda said. Her voice cracked. "I was asleep when it started." She told them as much as she could recall, though time and shock had disjointed her memories, making them unreal, as if her nightmares had become mixed with reality. Though she wondered what kind of reality. A reality in which a girl could erase the air from her lungs with a touch of her fingers? In which something or someone could burst into her flat and do what they'd done? In which someone could wreck a room and a human body within the space of a few seconds with the impact of a bomb? In which people could die of heart attacks because someone touched their chests?

When she had finished, Harridan sent the policewoman to fetch a drink for her.

"Just water, please," Miranda said. She felt as if she had drunk nothing for days.

While the woman was out of the room, the Inspector said, "We've had the autopsy results on the bodies found at the house yesterday."

"The heart attacks?"

"Heart attacks with collapsed lungs," he said. "Which intrigued me when you mentioned what happened to you when Lucilla touched your chest."

Miranda felt her skin grow cold – and an urge to be sick.

"None of this is real, is it?" she said. "I'm hallucinating, aren't I? This is some kind of asylum, not a police station at all?"

She felt a deep sense of dread seep through her, knowing that whatever had happened was real – all too real, she thought as she tried to blot the images of what she glimpsed inside the living room when the police took her away last night. The blood. The body parts. The dismembered head that had stared with sightless eyes from the blood-drenched floor at the end of the upended sofa.

Harridan stood up and walked to her side of the table; he placed a hand on her shoulder. "You know it's true," he told her. "So do I."

"Why am I here?" Miranda asked.

DI Butler said, "We don't intent to hold you. I had a word with Sergeant Harridan before the interview. Even though none of what happened makes sense, we don't believe you had anything to do with what happened to the girl. Why uniformed even put you in a cell last night, I don't know. I can only apologise. There wasn't a speck of blood on you or your clothes. Anyone could have seen that. Or should have done. Forensics confirmed it. Whoever killed the girl would have been drenched with blood."

Miranda looked away, unable to accept what had happened to Lucilla, even though her last feelings towards her had been fear.

"There's no way you could have been involved in attacking her," Harridan said. "You're free to go."

"Go where?" The thought of returning to her flat was too horrifying.

"Have you family or friends you could turn to?"

Miranda nodded. "I have my sister. She's married with kids. She'll put me up, even if it is the sofa." Though she knew Victoria would probably get two of the girls to share bedrooms. "I can sort something out."

"Ring from here. That's the least I can do." At that moment the policewoman arrived with a glass of water, which Miranda emptied in one.

It was midday by the time her sister arrived to drive her to her house. Within seconds of getting there, Miranda was whisked indoors, where a meal and something hot to drink were waiting for her.

"The kids are at school," Victoria said. "We have the house to ourselves till the brats coming charging in just after three. Bill gets back at six," Bill being her husband. Older and plumper than Miranda, Victoria seemed to have put aside her usual asperity and was full of concern for her sister's welfare instead. "Is there anything you need?"

Miranda shook her head as she sat on one of the over soft armchairs in the living room, one wall dominated by a plasma screen, computer games scattered about the deep pile carpet, sure signs of the girls' domination of the room. "The police brought me my handbag. I thought I might go out later and buy some clothes."

"How long before you can return to your flat?" Victoria asked.

"Heaven knows. That's up to the police. Though I don't know whether I could ever be able to live there again."

"I wouldn't blame you," Victoria said. She had already heard the news reports on the local radio station. "Lucky for you one of your neighbours rang the police."

"They must have thought there was a riot," Miranda said, though she had no desire to elaborate. Victoria had already asked if she wanted to talk about it, but Miranda had politely said no. "It's too horrible," she told her. "You wouldn't want to hear."

"When the kids are back, we'll go out together," Victoria said. "I'll drive us to the shops, and you can buy what you need. For goodness sake, Miranda, it'll take more than one pair of hands just to carry the bags."

Miranda smiled weakly. "Though I don't expect to go mad. I've only so much on my credit cards and I still have a wardrobe full of clothes at the flat."

"Never mind all of that," Victoria said. "You need something to take your mind off what's happened."

Miranda wondered how much she had guessed about Lucilla. Which made her want to cry, though she knew she shouldn't. She had barely known the girl much more than a week. She had known her as someone close for just a few days. A few days of craziness that had become even crazier at the end.

But why? And how?

She wondered if even the police would find out.

With an effort, Miranda agreed to Victoria's offer. Perhaps her presence and that of the girls would help to cheer her up, at least for the moment. Though she knew no matter what they did she would need more than tiredness tonight to sleep. And something stronger, she knew, than a bottle of wine.

A trip to Threshers would have to be on their schedule sometime today, surreptitious or otherwise, though Victoria surprised her later by suggesting they buy a bottle of vodka. "I prefer Absolute, straight from the freezer." She smiled with what Miranda could have sworn was such a look of empathy it made her wonder just how often her sister indulged herself.

By the time they returned to suburbia, Bill was home.

An overweight man, nearly six feet tall, he invariably reminded Miranda of a world-weary, overstuffed, balding teddy bear in his creased work suit. He gave her a brief, deep-felt hug.

"How are you managing?" His voice a sympathetic murmur, he regarded her with critical eyes. "I read all about it in tonight's paper. I could hardly believe it. You must be devastated."

By common understanding none of them talked about what had happened while the girls were about, especially the older, Daisy. At eight she had well developed ears that her mother said missed next to nothing. Little Wendy, six years old and podgy, with more energy than a hyperactive puppy, was in a world of her own, caring little about grown-up talk. Even so, what Miranda had gone through was so horrendous, none of them wanted to risk any of it leaking to the girls.

By nine the sisters were tucked in bed, their light turned out, and Victoria returned downstairs, looking tired. Miranda, with what happened last night, felt even more like sleep, though whenever she tried to rest her eyes the images that came to her drifting mind brought her back to consciousness with a sickening jolt, and she knew she would not find it easy tonight. When would she after what had happened? She knew from her work at the Shelter, many of whose residents had gone through harrowing, violent experiences, it could sometimes take years for the mental damage inflicted on them to be healed. If ever, she thought, knowing some who had gone beyond what even the finest therapy or drugs could do to repair.

She hoped what she saw and heard last night would one day fade, but for the moment it was so raw she knew she wouldn't sleep like she used to do for a long time to come.

Not without something to dull her senses, at least.

"Be a dear, fetch some glasses," Victoria said when she returned to the living room. She made a token effort at picking up some of the girls' toys, which she tossed onto an empty armchair, before slumping onto the sofa while Bill obediently wandered into the kitchen.

Victoria flung her head round to glance at Miranda. "Do you want to talk?" she asked, though her interest sounded forced to Miranda, who suspected she did not relish hearing what had happened.

"I'd rather drink first," Miranda said, knowing Bill would return with the vodka as well as some glasses.

Eventually, two downed vodkas and cokes inside her (heavy on the vodka and light on the coke) Miranda told them a little of what happened but refused to go into details. She also avoided telling them what seemed to happen when Lucilla touched her chest. They would think she was delusional if she told them that. Even she found it hard to believe any more, as if she had imagined it.

By eleven, her story told, Miranda could feel herself starting to doze. Perhaps the alcohol was beginning to work at last, she thought, aware that the aching in her head had gone for the first time since what happened in her flat.

"I've made Daisy's bed up for you," Victoria said. "You look bushed."

Miranda said that she was.

"Hopefully, I'll sleep through," she said. And not disturb anyone, she added to herself, hoping against hope she would have no nightmares. She finished her vodka, said goodnight, then headed for the stairs.

After visiting the bathroom, where she had a drink of water, she made her way into Daisy's room. She curled up on the bed and hugged the thick duvet around her. The child's bed was too short, and she had to bend her knees or leave her feet sticking out from under the covers, but that hardly mattered tonight. Lulled by the vodka, she quickly sank into an ever-deepening chasm of darkness. Images from last night still swam before her, but they seemed less focussed now, as if viewed through a foggy lens. Besides, her body was so tired even her agitated mind could do little to stem off sleep for long.

"Miranda."

For a moment she wasn't sure if she heard her name being called out or not.

Perhaps she had dreamed it.

She struggled to turn over in the cramped bed, with its thick, overly squashy child's mattress, to peer at the Disney Princess alarm clock on the chest of drawers beside the bed. It was two in the morning. Two fifteen, to be precise, Miranda corrected herself, wondering what had woken her. Other than her dreams, she thought as she tasted the stickiness of too much coke on her tongue and the acid burn of too much vodka in her liver.

"Miranda."

It was a soft voice. A girl's.

It sounded so much like…

Miranda gritted her teeth, knowing that she was wrong. Not now. Not after what had happened to Lucilla.

What had happened to her body.

Miranda looked across the room. The door onto

the landing was ajar. The lights outside were on, showing the small figure in silhouette.

It was Daisy.

Had the girl wandered here by mistake, on her way back from the bathroom?

"What's the matter, Daisy?" Miranda asked, puzzled at the girl missing "Auntie" from her name. In the Raywood household that was something neither of the girls would ever do. Not in Victoria's hearing. Nor Bill's either, Miranda thought, a stickler for family protocols.

"I need your help, Miranda."

This time she felt a shiver run through her, chilling her skin, as she realised this wasn't Daisy's voice.

"Lucilla?"

The girl stepped nearer.

Miranda recognised Daisy. She could see her face, even in the gloom. Besides, she was far too small for Lucilla, crazy though she knew that was. Lucilla was dead. Dismembered. Her body ripped into a hundred pieces.

But the voice was hers. She knew that with certainty.

The fear that filled her as she stared at the girl made it impossible for her to move. Miranda's will seemed paralysed, and all she could do was stare.

"Daisy!"

The door opened wider and Victoria stood behind the girl, a dressing gown hung around her pale pink nightie.

"What are you disturbing your auntie for, Daisy?

Have you forgotten you're sleeping with your sister, silly?"

She bustled in, putting her hands on Daisy's shoulders.

"I'm sorry about this, Miranda. She must be confused."

At which Miranda felt some of the fear seep from her body, restored by the normality of Victoria's presence.

"That's all right," Miranda said. "No harm done."

Victoria smiled as she guided Daisy back to the door.

Though it was hours before Miranda could compose herself enough to sleep once more.

That voice had been so much like Lucilla's.

She felt a grinding ache in the pit of her stomach when she remembered it, ridiculous though she knew it was. She must have been mistaken. That was obvious. Logic, reason, common-sense, call it what you will, Miranda told herself, made this the only explanation.

She had to have been mistaken.

Next morning, tired from hardly sleeping most of the night, Miranda was relieved to see the children had already been taken to school by the time she wandered into the kitchen, partly drawn by the smell of coffee percolating. Bill had also gone.

Fresh from having just returned from the school run, Victoria was eating a bowl of muesli. She greeted Miranda with a cheerful smile.

"I hope Daisy didn't ruin your sleep," she said.

"Not at all," Miranda lied. She poured some coffee into a mug. "Do you have any paracetamol?"

"Hangover?"

"No worse than normal," Miranda said, acknowledge-ing to herself that even before what happened she had begun to drink too much. Was this going to tip her over the edge, she wondered, into something worse? As well as being a wife-beater their father had been an alcoholic. That he died from sclerosis of the liver, was something their mother had never tired of lecturing them about whenever either of them took a drink or, God forbid, got drunk.

"I never start the day without one," Victoria confessed. She reached into a drawer for a cardboard packet. "Ibuprofen usually sorts me out." She passed Miranda two of them.

"Was mother right?" Miranda asked. "Is it our genes?"

Victoria laughed. "You can't blame everything on Daddy. I didn't drink till Bill started to bore me senseless." She shrugged as if it was nothing of importance. "It's not his fault. He means well. But you've heard him, Miranda. Since the girls were born it's as if he's aged. He's more like their grandfather than their dad."

"How was Daisy this morning?" Miranda asked, unsure if she should.

"Her usual self. Why? Did she worry you last night?"

"Not really. I'm not surprised she forgot I was in her room. She looked half asleep."

Victoria laughed. "I think she was still a bit shamefaced about it this morning. Certainly made her quieter than usual."

"Quieter?"

"She's a bit of a chatterbox. Surely you've noticed? Never stops talking given half a chance. It's a wonder poor Wendy gets a word in edgeways, poor mite."

"Not today?"

"No, not today. Probably a bit off colour. But you'll see, she'll be running on all pistons by the time she gets home. Natter, natter, natter. You'll miss that peace and quiet then."

Miranda hoped her sister was right as she swallowed her pills, washing them down with the last dregs of coffee.

Later that morning the doorbell rang. When Victoria answered it, she ushered in Sergeant Harridan.

"Sorry to disturb you," the policeman said as he was shown into the living room. He sat down facing the two sisters. "I'm here to update you on our investigations so far." He shuffled his feet for a moment, then said, "There's also the matter of a discrepancy in what you told me on the phone several days ago, Miss Walters, when you denied any knowledge of where the girl Lucilla had gone after she left the Shelter. It's obvious she was living with you, yet you told me you didn't know where she was."

Miranda had been expecting this. "I couldn't tell you," she said. "I was concerned about my job. I'd already told my boss she had gone."

"Your boss being Mary Milligan. Who died from a heart attack two days ago?"

"Mary died?" Victoria asked, surprised. "You never said, Miranda."

"With what's happened since…"

"With what's happened since," Harridan said, "I suppose one more death is easy to forget." He coughed into his fist. "There are several questions I need to ask about Mary Milligan." The policeman leaned forward and looked Miranda in the eye with a shrewd, calculating expression which she found disconcerting. His previous friendliness seemed to have gone and she was aware of an air of suspicion about him. "Like all the recent heart attacks, a medical examination of her body found her lungs had collapsed. The coroner is baffled. Other than this, Miss Milligan appears to have been in perfect health. No signs of anything that could have caused heart problems for her." He said this flatly. "Though there are a few things that bother me more," he said. "Even though she was found inside her car, we're certain she did not die there. Fibres found on her clothes match those of the carpet inside your flat, Miss Walters. In fact, they're spread over her clothes so much she must have been lying on it. We found strands of hair too – strands matching those of the girl Lucilla." Harridan paused for a moment, then said, "Did Mary Milligan die at your flat, Miss Walters? Did you and the girl move her body, carry it to her car then drive it to where she was found?" After a moment's silence, he said, "There are fibres from your clothes inside the car. If we took samples of your hair would we find those too?"

Realising it would be pointless to deny what the sergeant said, Miranda nodded. She heard Victoria's astonished, disbelieving gasp. But what was the point of lying now? Lucilla was dead. Miranda knew her career at the Shelter was over. After what the police had discovered she would never be allowed to work there again.

"Why?" Victoria whispered. "Why did you do it?"

Miranda wondered about that too. It seemed madness now, though they might have got away with it if Lucilla had not been murdered, she thought. At which something she had hitherto tried to ignore came back to her: what was it that murdered her? What was it that smashed its way through the door into her flat and killed her?

"What attacked Lucilla?" Miranda said, knowing, for all her lies, there was nothing the police could use to blame her for anything that happened to the girl. "I might have been stupid in letting her stay with me and in lying to Mary – and to you – but I didn't kill her."

Harridan agreed. "You were stupid," he said. "And you could have got yourself into a lot of trouble. But we know you didn't kill her. Who did?" He shrugged. "And how did whoever killed her get into your room through the window?"

"It was like some kind of devil," Miranda said, knowing she sounded ridiculous. Feeling ridiculous too.

"If I wasn't a confirmed materialist, I might agree with you," the policeman said. "Except there are traces of DNA: scraps of material, some of it skin, splinters that might have been claws. They're all being investigated. We should have results that will tell us what it was soon."

"*What* it was?" Victoria said.

Harridan looked embarrassed for a moment. "A slip of the tongue."

The two sisters exchanged glances, and Miranda could see Victoria was far from convinced it was a slip at all.

"From what my sister has told me," Victoria said, "it was more like some kind of animal. What else could have done it?"

Harridan frowned. "I can't speculate. Till we get some evidence, I know no more than you. All I would ask," he said to Miranda, "is that if you know anything about the girl – who she was, where she came from, who she associated with – tell me. We've checked her DNA and her fingerprints, but nothing's turned up yet. We've still no idea who she was."

"Nor do I," Miranda said. "She wouldn't talk about herself."

"But you allowed her to share your flat?"

Miranda shook her head. "I know, I was crazy. I don't know why I did it. I really, really don't." Which she didn't, she knew. It was as if she had thrown caution to the wind, trusting her home, her possessions, her career to a girl who shared nothing of herself with her. Why she had trusted her she did not know. It was madness.

Almost as mad as the way in which Lucilla was killed.

"If you do remember something," the policeman said, "contact me. We're trying to help. And anything you tell us might help catch whoever did it."

Though Miranda wondered whether even Detective Sergeant Mike Harridan really believed that.

After he had gone, Victoria went for the vodka.

"I know – it's ridiculously early, but I need it today," she said as she placed two glasses on the table.

Her nerves jangled by the policeman's visit, Miranda was only too glad to agree. "What about the girls?" she asked. "Aren't you supposed to pick them up at three?"

Victoria pouted. "I'll walk. It'll do them good to use their legs for once. It's less than two miles anyway. Not exactly a marathon."

Though Miranda wondered whether her sister would feel the same way when she had to trek it.

In the end they had two glasses each, before Victoria decided to make some lunch. As they drank and ate Miranda unfolded more of what had happened over the past two weeks, telling her sister far more than she would have said had Bill been there. For the most part Victoria seemed to accept what she heard at face value, only interjecting now and then for a more detailed explanation or expressing anything like scepticism.

When it came to what happened when Lucilla was killed, Victoria asked how sure she was of what she remembered.

"Couldn't someone have broken into your flat without you realising it? Could that have happened?" Victoria asked.

Miranda shook her head. "Not if what I remember is right."

"You were asleep, Miranda, probably half cut from the wine you'd been drinking, in a state of shock at the window being broken and what happened next. How much can you rely on what you remember?"

"Put like that, not much," Miranda said, trying to clarify her memories, but as each day passed, they seemed to be more blurred, jumbling into nothing clearer than the recollections of a nightmare. Look at last night, she thought. When she was woken by Daisy after only drinking a few glasses of vodka she could have sworn the girl spoke with Lucilla's voice. Even worse, she'd been certain for a moment it really was Lucilla who was talking to her, even though she could see who it was, as if sight and sound had their own realities. As if her own mind was creating its own realities, she added, knowing this was probably nearer the truth.

"The best thing now," Victoria said, "is to put all this behind you. Find yourself a new job, a new flat, a new life."

Easier said than done, Miranda thought, but she said nothing, just nodded her head. Perhaps her sister was right. How long would it take her, though, with more visits from the police and more questions to be answered – or evaded?

At half two Victoria said she had better set off for school to be in time to meet the girls when they came out. She asked if Miranda would like to go with her. It was a fine day, the air cold but clear, with a powdery blue sky and barely more than a breeze.

"It'll do you good," Victoria said.

At the prospect of idling inside the house on her own with only daytime TV as a poor companion, Miranda said, "Why not?"

She felt befuddled from the drinks they'd had, and some fresh air would help clear her head. Donning coats and gloves, they set off at a brisk walk, Miranda finding she was actually enjoying the exercise. A fresh start, she thought. That really is what I need. Less booze as well, half regretting already the vodkas they'd drunk. She could still remember the papery yellow skin of their father in the final months of life, his liver useless by then. She was never sure whether most of his anguish was over the imminence of his death, the pains and illness of his body or his inability to drink anymore. He had often begged her to bring him some whisky. "Just a small one, girl, that's all I need." Till in the end she did.

He died the next day.

Another layer of guilt on her conscience, to which

she had added how many more in the past two weeks?

It was a relief when they finally saw the school. It had been a good walk, though the air was a tad too chill for them to talk much on the way. Now the grey stone walls and black-painted iron railings of St Paul's Primary School were only a block away. Cars were already parked along the road as mothers and sometimes fathers too arrived for their offspring. A lollypop lady tried her best to control the traffic, but some parents were too impatient to reach the disappearing parking spaces around the school and Miranda was amazed no one was killed.

"Is this what you have to put up with every day?" Miranda asked.

"Crazy, isn't it? We're all as bad as each other, though. Me included," she said with a grin.

Somewhere, muffled by thick stone walls, a bell began to ring.

"Here they come," Victoria said. "There'll be bedlam now."

Though it was far less chaotic than the arrival of the parental cars had been, as pupils streamed from the building, bags and satchels swinging through the air. The two women moved nearer the gates so Daisy and Wendy would see them when they emerged.

The first to arrive was Wendy, running and weaving between larger, older children.

"Mummy! Mummy! Mummy!" She grasped a wrinkled sheet of paper in one hand, which Miranda saw was a watercolour painting with the obligatory one-inch strip of blue at the top for the sky, a yellow sun radiating splashes of light, and a stick-figure in the middle which she did not need to guess was meant to be her mother.

Victoria held it in both hands, admiring what her daughter had painted while Wendy gaspingly told her all about it. And for one moment Miranda felt a twinge of envy. At thirty, though, she wasn't too old one day to have a Wendy of her own, she told herself. All she had to do was to stop regarding every man she met as a selfish sarcastic brute like their father.

That was all, she thought, knowing just how tough that would be. Not helped by the bad experiences she'd had when she'd tried to ignore her doubts. Perhaps she just couldn't see what a bastard some men were till it was too late. Or fail to see those who weren't when she met them.

Victoria showed her the picture, her pride in what her daughter had daubed across the thick sheet of coarse paper brimming over. "Well done, Wendy, well done."

Miranda glanced at her watch. By now ten minutes had passed and most of the other groups of parents and their offspring had begun to disappear. Even the traffic snarl up had almost unravelled itself.

She saw Victoria glance apprehensively at the school.

"You don't suppose she's been kept back for some reason?" Miranda said.

Victoria shook her head. "She has her mobile.

She'd have rung by now if she has."

Just then they saw her, heading their way, hands folded across her chest, head down.

"She was impossible this morning," Victoria confided as they watched Daisy thread as close to the wall as she could between groups of children still hanging around, waiting. "I virtually had to order her into the car. I swear she wanted me to bring it even closer to the door if I could. The little madam."

"Is she often like that?"

"Never. It was as if she was frightened of going outside." She shook her head. "I suppose they all get phases."

Miranda watched as Daisy drew nearer. The girl looked up from staring at her feet, her eyes scanning the length of the road, obviously searching for sight of her mother's car. As soon as she saw them stood there Miranda was sure a look of dismay flooded her face. The girl ran towards them, scattering other pupils out of her way.

"Where is it?" she all but shouted at her mother, clinging to her, her words bursting from her mouth in near hysteria.

"We've walked," Victoria said, plainly astonished at the reaction. "It'll do us good to use our legs for once."

"No!" the girl shouted. "I can't. We mustn't."

"It's too late for that." Victoria's voice was surprisingly calm, though there was an edge to it. "I'm not walking all that way to drive back and pick you up just because you don't want to walk. Now stop being silly."

Miranda saw a look of irritation on her sister's face.

"Do you want to hold my hand?" Miranda asked the girl.

Daisy looked up at her. There was confusion in her eyes, and Miranda wondered whether the girl even understood her own fears. She glanced around the street. Miranda noticed she looked upwards too, as if she were worried about the branches of the trees along the kerb. Miranda held out her hand. Daisy sidled forwards, keeping close to the school wall, then reached up and grasped it.

Obviously mimicking her older sister, with a huge grin Wendy took hold of her mother's hand and together they started off home, though Miranda winced at the tightness of Daisy's grip on her fingers. She looked down at her now and then, each time seeing Daisy's eyes staring back at hers, their intensity startling.

So much like Lucilla's, Miranda thought, her stomach clenching with apprehension. Was her grasp on reality so loose she was starting to imagine impossible things like this? Lucilla was dead, she told herself. She had to accept that, however much she had somehow begun to love the girl in her final days. In her imagination she could see her butchered remains on the mortuary slab, photographed, examined, and catalogued, every detail of the damage inflicted on them written up for the police and their investigation. With all that had happened Miranda knew she could not afford to break down now. Whoever killed Lucilla was still out there, she told herself.

Whatever that was, Miranda thought, pursing her brows when she tried to remember what she saw of the attacker. And the sounds. The horrible, terrible ripping sounds. The bangs and crashes.

Miranda looked down at Daisy's eyes in her solemn, frightened, pallid face. They were just the child's eyes, she rebuked herself. Nothing more. Not Lucilla's – Daisy's.

But why had Daisy started to fear the outdoors?

Why did she come to her room last night and say, "Miranda… I need your help, Miranda"?

Why did her face remind her so much of Lucilla's, though the two were so dissimilar?

Miranda was relieved when they arrived back home. The girls were bundled indoors, where Daisy seemed to recover from her "bout of nerves", as Victoria called it, running upstairs to the room she was sharing with Wendy.

"I don't know what's come over the girl," Victoria said. "It'll pass. These things always do, so I've heard," she added with a rueful smile. "She's entering that age when they start to act peculiar now and then."

Miranda smiled and said nothing. There was nothing she could say that her sister would either want to hear or choose to believe. Not that she wanted to believe any of it either. Far too much had happened over the past few days that didn't make sense. What she needed was peace and normality now. Loads of normality, she thought, longingly, as humdrum, as commonplace, as boring as possible, please help me God.

Though there was little that was more humdrum, commonplace or boring than Bill, who arrived home at six looking tired as usual. Victoria told him about their visit from the police as they sat in the kitchen, drinking coffee, though it was obvious he didn't relish listening to any of it, none of which fitted his narrow world of work and watching TV. A world Miranda envied now – which had been very much her own, she realised, a short while ago, an insight that shocked her a little. Had she been so much like Bill? she wondered, before she remembered that her work had been out in the real world dealing with real problems, with women who had suffered at the hands (and fists) of abusive partners. When she returned home at night, the escape into wine and watching TV was at least excusable. What was Bill's? Escape from the boredom of his accountancy office?

Miranda turned away from them. She had no right to criticise Bill, she knew. Not now. Not after the way she had made such a mess of things.

If she had done what Mary Milligan had told her Lucilla would have been sent on to another Shelter and might still be alive. Mary might still be alive as well. And she would have a job. And a flat. And a life of her own.

"Perhaps I should move out," she said after tea when she and Victoria were clearing away the dishes and Bill and the girls were in the living room, watching a DVD.

Victoria looked at her in astonishment. "Don't be ridiculous. Have we made you unwelcome?"

"Not at all," Miranda said.

"Then why?"

"I don't know. I'm not sure. Except," she said, "I feel as if I'm involving you all in something you would be better off without."

"What nonsense," Victoria said. "We're family. I'm sure you'd stand by us if we had problems you could help us with. It's little enough we're doing anyway, offering you a bed."

"You're offering me more than that. I don't feel I deserve it after what's happened. You're giving me a place in your family, which means more to me than anything else. I just hope," she added, unable to hide the worry from her voice, "I don't let you down."

Scoffing at the very idea, Victoria took her sister in her arms. "I'll let you know soon enough if you let us down. That's what older sisters are for. But I don't think you will."

Miranda hoped she was right, but her doubts would not let go.

At first Miranda tried to resist the temptation to have more alcohol that night but, after the girls had gone to bed, Victoria opened a bottle of wine. Just one glass, Miranda thought. Her shoulders felt tense and the sight of her sister and brother-in-law enjoying the wine was too much for her. Though it always had been, she knew, as she took her first sip and felt some of the stiffness melt away.

Before long, Bill began to doze, chin pressed against his chest, one hand still firmly gripping his empty glass.

Victoria glanced at him.

"No staying power," she said, refilling hers and Miranda's glasses. "Then again, we Walters girls have always had good heads for drink. Remember when I used to take you to the pub with the gang?" The "gang" being Victoria's closest friends from sixth form college, then in their final year, while Miranda was in her last year at school, though already she looked as old as the others if she applied enough makeup. Miranda had tagged along with them, Victoria surreptitiously adding the odd stiff drink to her cokes. And though their mother had always abhorred them coming home the worse for drink, they were perhaps the only times either of them got anything approaching appreciation from their father.

Like father like daughters, Miranda thought. Why fight it?

Not that she felt like fighting it now. The more they drank, the more she knew she wanted to, if only because it helped blunt the sharpness of whatever she felt over what had happened. Dulled the senses. Becalmed her conscience.

Made everything that much easier to ignore.

Or forget.

They avoided the news on TV. Too much time was still being spent on the horrors that happened at Miranda's flat, even if most of it was only on the regional news.

"Thank Christ no reporters have found out about you being here," Victoria said, though Miranda knew it was only a matter of time.

"What'll we do if they do find out I'm here?" Miranda asked. "We can't subject the girls to that, especially when their friends at school hear about it."

So far, the only reference to Miranda had been that a girl's body had been found murdered in "a flat belonging to a social worker" who was not suspected of being involved in what happened. *So far*, Miranda thought to herself, though she knew she wasn't beyond suspicion despite the lack of evidence to show she had been *physically* involved in it.

"It's not been long since it happened," Miranda went on. "Give them time and even the *Evening Chronicle* will come knocking at your door."

"Much good that will do them," Victoria said with the conviction four large glasses of wine had already instilled her with.

"I'm serious," Miranda rebuked her. "It'll take more than just telling them to bugger off."

"That's a start, why knock it?"

The sisters laughed, though Miranda's humour felt forced, knowing the true test of sisterly support would come when this happened. That would perhaps be a good time to drive away to avoid all of this, taking some of the heat from Victoria and her family. She still had enough credit on her cards to afford to hide away for several months. Miranda glanced towards the glass-panelled door into the hallway. Through the dappled panes she could see the stairs, up which, hopefully, Daisy would be asleep by now. She was worried about the girl, especially after the way she had begun to behave. How much worse would she be if she heard about the murder at her aunt's flat? Miranda would either become a figure of shame in Daisy's eyes or be transmogrified into some mysterious celebrity. Whatever happened, Miranda knew she would never be looked at by Daisy as the same safe, dependable, comfortable aunt she had been in the past, and she regretted this – something else she would lose because of her decision to take Lucilla to her flat. Were the few days of happiness she enjoyed with that girl worth all of this, she wondered, regretting it more than anything else she had ever done in her life?

"Was there a noise upstairs?" Victoria asked.

Miranda heard it too, perhaps one of the girls groaning in her sleep. She put down her glass. "I'll check," she said before Victoria could move. "It'll only take a second and I need the loo anyway," she added as an excuse.

She shut the living room door behind her, before hurrying upstairs. The air felt cold – unnaturally cold – despite the central heating. Miranda's pulse raced as she neared the landing. Not again, she thought, feeling the desperation of her plea, please God not again.

On the landing she paused. Even the lights looked dim along it. Or was she imagining things yet again? She hoped so, though her heart was still racing, and she felt so afraid she almost didn't want to go any further. Then she heard it. And she was certain now that one of the girls was moaning.

As quietly as she could, her nerves on edge, Miranda opened the door into their bedroom. In the gloom she could see Wendy was still asleep. Daisy, though, had kicked off her duvet and was rolling about from side to side. Miranda tiptoed towards her, laying a hand on her shoulders.

"Hush," she whispered. "It's all right. You're only dreaming."

Daisy stopped moving at once except to turn her head towards Miranda, her eyes wide open. Even in the darkness they looked alarmingly bright as if an inner light was shining behind them.

"Don't leave," the girl said. Her voice was quiet but insistent, trembling with fear.

"No one's going to leave," Miranda said. "Your parents are only downstairs. They'll be going to bed soon. And I'll only be a few feet away down the landing." Even as she spoke, she could feel her own nervousness. The girl's voice had sounded so much like Lucilla's it was uncanny. She tried to convince herself she was mistaken but she knew that she wasn't.

"You know, don't you," the girl whispered. It was not a question, and Miranda felt as if the air had become even colder. "You know who I am, Miranda."

"That's impossible."

"Nothing is impossible."

Miranda straightened. Most of her wanted to rush from the room. She didn't want any more of this insane nightmare. Lucilla was dead, she told herself. And this was Daisy. Her niece. Her sister's child.

"If you let me down," the girl said, "it will be worse for everyone."

"Worse?" Miranda felt frightened and weak, certain she was having a mental breakdown. It was the only explanation.

"You must take me away from here – in your car. We must go away as far as we can from here."

Miranda shook her head. "How? Why? I don't understand."

"Later tonight, when they're asleep, I'll come to your room. I'll be dressed. Make sure you are too."

"And then?"

"We leave. Bring your car as close to the house as you can. I can't afford to be outside. You remember what happened at your flat?"

Miranda gasped. "Lucilla?"

The girl stared steadily at her. "If you don't want your sister and her family to suffer – like I did…" The girl closed her eyes. "Be ready," she whispered. "We must leave tonight."

Miranda stood by the bed a few moments more, uncertain, knowing she should go down and tell Victoria what her daughter had said. What would happen if she did? Wouldn't Victoria think she was making things up? She would never believe Daisy said any of this. It was too bizarre, crazy. She wasn't even sure if she believed it herself.

When she left the room Miranda returned downstairs, uncertain over what to say – or not to say – to her sister.

"Everything okay?" Victoria asked.

Feeling guilty, Miranda said it was quiet upstairs. "One of them must've been having a bad dream," she said. She sat down and reached for her wine, then hesitated. Should she drink any more if she was likely to be driving away from here in a few hours? *If* she was going to drive away, she thought. *If*. She had to think this through, she told herself, but how and when? Victoria wanted to talk, and her inconsequential chatter distracted Miranda from what she really, desperately needed to think about.

"I'm not feeling well," Miranda said suddenly. She put down her glass. "I think I'll have an early night."

"Is there anything I can get you? Some tablets?" Victoria asked. Her concern upset Miranda, who felt like she was about to betray her and her family. She shook her head.

"I'll be all right. Nothing a good night's sleep won't put right."

"If you're sure?"

Miranda nodded this time. "I'm sure," though she wished, fervently, that she was as she left the room and went upstairs. Inside her room, she sat on the edge of the small bed. Daisy's bed. How much of the real Daisy was still inside the girl, she wondered, certain now the girl must have been possessed by Lucilla, by her dead spirit, in a way she could not understand – which made her wonder whether Lucilla had been possessed as well. Had she been taken over just as Daisy had been? It was a ridiculous thought, she knew, but what other explanation was there? None of it made any sense to her down-to-earth, practical, sceptical side, except that she knew something she could not describe had somehow crashed through the window of her flat only two nights ago and attacked Lucilla, killing her. She had sensed, perhaps even half seen the thing. She had smelt it, she knew; she would never forget the stench, that stink of mould and decay. Or the sounds that battered her ears as it all but filled the room with its onslaught.

That had been so insane only something equally insane could explain it.

Miranda cupped her head in her hands and sobbed, wondering what had happened to her life. It was a terrible nightmare, and she would have been relieved if she could have convinced herself it was just the sickness of her mind, that she had imagined it all. But Lucilla had been killed. Her dismembered body had been scattered all over her bedroom. She had glimpsed it once and would never forget the terrible sight. That was not her imagination, she knew. None of it was. Insane or not, it was real.

Just as she was sure that Lucilla's voice had been real when Daisy spoke to her.

Miranda knew she could not ignore what the girl had said, whether she liked what she was about to do or not.

6

She listened to Victoria, then Bill as they climbed the stairs, their voices low. She heard the light switches being turned off, then an even lower mumble of voices from her sister's bedroom, before eventual silence. Still Miranda sat on the edge of her bed, listening to the creaks and groans of the central heating pipes as they started to cool. She listened to the wind outside her bedroom window. As the quiet intensified she even listened to the sound of her pulse as it throbbed through her temples. She had begun to feel thirsty as the effects of the few glasses of wine she'd drunk began to dissipate. She would still be over the legal alcohol limit, she knew, but she could drive reliably enough not to attract the attention of the police.

Which was when she realised, she was going to do what Lucilla said.

As quietly as she could she filled a bag with what few possessions she had with her, zipping it shut, then leaving it, ready, on the bed. As the air cooled, she put on a denim coat and a scarf. She sat down again, her light still on, and stared at the door.

Over two hours passed while she waited, before the door opened. Daisy stood on the landing, already dressed, a bag in one hand. She wore her weekend clothes, with a hooded cagoule.

Without talking, they crept downstairs, Daisy leading the way. The hallway felt warmer than

Miranda's bedroom, which made the outside air seem even colder when she unlocked the front door and stepped out onto the concrete path. Her car was still stood by the kerb. She'd left it there because there wasn't room along with Bill's and Victoria's on the drive.

She turned to Daisy. "I can't bring my car any closer to the door. Your father's is in the way."

"You know he isn't my father; Victoria isn't my mother either," the girl said. "You should get used to calling me Lucilla again. Daisy isn't with us now; not fully anyway."

Miranda felt chilled at the lack of concern in Lucilla's voice, as if Daisy were inconsequential, a negligible necessity.

The girl glanced down the avenue, then up at the sky. She shivered.

"Unlock your car and call me when you're ready."

Unsure why she was obediently doing what the girl told her, Miranda hurried to the road, unlocked her car, then climbed inside. It felt as if she had stepped into a fridge. She lowered the passenger window and called, "Now," as quietly as she could.

Lucilla raced down the path and threw herself onto the passenger seat, slamming the door shut behind her.

"Where to?" Miranda asked.

"Just away." The girl's eyes were intent on taking in as much as she could of their surroundings as they drove off. Miranda could feel her nervousness.

There was little traffic as they drove through town and took the road towards the motorway.

"South," the girl said.

"How far?"

"As far as possible. I'll tell you when." The girl folded her arms across her chest, scrunching even deeper into her seat so that she looked even smaller than ever. Miranda glanced at her, wondering what hold she had on her. Miranda knew Victoria would ring the police as soon as she found they had both gone missing. How would she ever be able to explain to her sister why she had done it? She knew Victoria would never forgive her, especially after all the help she had given. What an ungrateful slap in the face this was. Miranda glanced at Daisy, unable to understand how the girl had been able to convince her to do this. Had it been how Lucilla had persuaded her to let her stay at her flat to start with, even though Miranda knew how wrong that was, how it would endanger her career at the Refuge?

What kind of control had the girl got over her? Love? Sex? Or something more?

Miranda gritted her teeth, half convinced she should turn back now or head for the nearest police station, pathetic though her story would sound if she tried to explain what had happened. It would only take Lucilla to burst into tears and no one would ever believe anything Miranda said.

She knew her options were limited. And the further she drove the more limited they would be.

"Why are you doing this to me?" Miranda asked. She saw Daisy look towards her.

"I have to," the girl said. "I need your help," then closed her eyes. And Miranda knew she would get no more from her. Reticent as ever, Lucilla was as tight-lipped as a clam. And Miranda knew she had no choice but to keep on driving. And hope that things would somehow, in some way work out.

By dawn she was exhausted. Bleary-eyed, knowing she was in danger of falling asleep at the wheel, Miranda drove onto the next motorway service station they reached. As she pulled up in one of the parking slots, the girl opened her eyes.

"I need a rest," Miranda said. "I need coffee. I need something to eat." Though whether she would be able to hold anything down she was not sure. She would probably throw up as soon as she ate it.

"I'll wait in the car," the girl said.

"Do you want me to bring you something? Some milk? A coke? Something to eat?"

Miranda took the girl's silence as no. Feeling even less sure why she was doing what Lucilla told her, Miranda climbed out and wandered through the dull pre-dawn gloom towards the service station, its neon lights far from comforting.

The place was quiet. The few motorists there were looked apathetic, some heading for the toilets, while others milled about the self-service restaurant which looked as if it had only just opened. There was, though, the smell of hot food. Its effect on Miranda was twofold. Her hunger craved it, but the awful tension in her stomach rebelled, and by the time she had a tray in her hand she finally settled on a couple of slices of toast and a mug of coffee. "A large mug," she said to the girl at the checkout.

Miranda took her tray to a table near the plate glass window where she could see her car. The girl was visible inside it, slumped so low it was as if she was hiding. Perhaps she was, Miranda thought, struggling to nibble her way through a slice of toast. It was warm and buttery and made her queasy, though she knew she needed something to eat. She washed it down with a sip of the coffee, hoping it would counteract her nausea.

After forcing herself to eat most of one slice, Miranda finally gave up and concentrated instead on the coffee, when her mobile started to ring. She reached inside her coat, at the same time feeling an impulse to throw up everything she had eaten. Even before she looked at the mobile's screen, she knew it was her sister. For several seconds she stared at Victoria's name while the phone continued its idiotic tune, undecided whether to answer it or not, knowing there was nothing she could say to her sister to explain what she had done. Abruptly, angry at herself, Miranda cancelled the call and switched the mobile off. There was nothing she could say – nothing at all.

Pushing herself to her feet, Miranda hurried back to her car.

"What's the matter?" the girl asked as Miranda

slammed the door shut behind her and reached for the keys.

"Your mother rang on my mobile." Miranda stared hard at the girl, searching for a reaction.

"Daisy's mother was certain to ring," the girl said. "Did you speak to her?" Miranda shook her head. "She'll ring the police. She knows your car, its make, its registration. They'll be looking for it."

Miranda felt herself panicking again, even though part of her wanted the police to catch them. At least then it would all be over.

Or would it?

"There is somewhere we can go," the girl said. "It isn't far."

Miranda stared at her. "How could you know that? Do you even know where we are?"

The girl's face showed the faintest of smiles. "Of course, I do."

And Miranda believed her. Crazy though it seemed she didn't doubt that the girl knew exactly where they were.

"I feel sick," Miranda said. "I need the toilets."

Lucilla smiled, as if amused at Miranda's weakness.

"Don't take long."

Miranda staggered from the car. She did feel sick. The more she listened to Lucilla's voice from her niece's lips, the more she realised how stupid she had been. She had carried that parasite to her sister's house and let it take the girl over. That she hadn't realised what would happen when she went there made no difference to her feelings of guilt. She should have realised something might happen, Miranda was sure, no matter how outlandish it seemed. The signs were there. Miranda could see them now when she looked back over what had happened since she first met Lucilla.

Miranda hurried inside the service station. As soon as she was out of sight of the car, she changed direction for the bridge that would take her to the other side of the motorway. She walked as fast as she could without drawing too much attention to herself.

As soon as she reached the other side of the motorway, she went to the exit. The filling station was a few hundred yards away and she hoped all the things she had decided she would need to end this nightmare were there.

In a way, rushing from one side of the motorway to the other helped her when she finally returned to the car. Her flushed face must have convinced Lucilla she was genuinely ill, because the girl's smile barely changed when she saw her. Miranda slumped behind the steering wheel, her heart still pounding. Beneath her coat she could feel her purchases pressing hard against her stomach. In one hand she held a half full bottle of coke. She looked at Lucilla.

"Would you like some?"

It was hot inside the car and she knew the girl would be thirsty. Whatever else she might be, the body she was in one was human, with all its frailties.

Miranda upended the bottle to her mouth to show that its contents were safe. She took a long drink then offered it to the girl. She saw Lucilla lick her lips, then reach for the bottle.

"Thanks," the girl said, before drinking from it. The coke was still icy, and Miranda knew what its impact would be on her thirst. Within a few moments the bottle had been drained.

Miranda turned the ignition, reversed out of their parking slot and drove towards the motorway slip road. She had drunk less of the coke than the girl probably thought. A mouthful at most. Lucilla had drunk the rest, in which Miranda had dissolved some of her Nytol tablets. They wouldn't automatically make the girl sleep, but they would make her drowsy. After being awake all night, Miranda hoped they would relax her enough she would fall asleep soon, especially if she raised the heating inside the car.

Several miles later, Miranda glanced at the girl. Already her eyes were starting to shut, and she could tell that Lucilla was having difficulty staying awake. Feeling tired as well, Miranda knew that if it hadn't been for the amount of attention she had to focus on driving she might well be nodding off too. That and tension at what she had planned. She felt afraid and nauseous. But she knew there was no choice. Not if she was going to make amends to her sister for what had happened.

A few minutes later she saw what she had been looking for, a police slip road used by patrol cars to park off the motorway.

Dropping into third, she drove towards it along the hard shoulder. Despite the noise as the tyres ground across the rougher surface Lucilla slept on. Miranda drove up the short incline that swung off the motorway towards the short, flattened summit. She was surprised at the depth of view this gave. She felt exposed up here, till she reminded herself those driving by would have to crane their necks to see her. It was ideally positioned for the police to have an unobstructed view of the motorway. It was also ideal for concealing them from sight.

Miranda put the car into neutral, pulled the handbrake, then quietly pushed her door open and slid outside. From under her coat she unwound the length of rubber hose she bought at the service station. Kneeling down, she forced one end onto the exhaust. The hot metal softened the rubber, making it easier to move. When Miranda was satisfied that she had pushed enough on so it wouldn't slip free, she took the other end of the pipe and passed it though the gap she had left in the rear door window. She wound up the window till it gripped the pipe, then slammed the door shut.

Lucilla awoke with a jolt.

She looked around, instantly taking in what Miranda had done and reached for her door handle, but Miranda had expected this and had already run around the car, using her weight to stop her from opening the door. Lucilla struggled against her, but an eight-year old's muscles were far too weak against the weight of Miranda's body as she leaned against the door panel. Even outside, Miranda could smell the exhaust fumes that were choking up the car's interior. Anger and fear filled Lucilla's face. She slammed her fists against the window.

"Let me out," she shouted.

Miranda shook her head. "This ends here."

Lucilla scrambled over the seats in a desperate attempt to reach the driver's door, but Miranda got there first. She stared through the window as the girl leaned against the door.

"You'll kill your niece," Lucilla shouted at her.

"You're killing her already."

Lucilla stared at her and Miranda could tell the girl realised how determined she was.

Which was when she felt it – a nasty, brutal scratching sensation inside her skull.

Miranda gasped as the sensation grew stronger. Lucilla was slipping into her head more blatantly this time. There was no pretence at hiding inside her, of waiting till a weaker victim was available. There was no finesse in what Lucilla was doing. It was rough, almost rape, as she grappled deep inside Miranda's mind. She could feel her gouging through her consciousness like something old, reptilian, foul and decrepit.

She could taste decay inside her throat.

It filled her lungs with its stench.

But Miranda was no immature child, easy to

manipulate. She was a grown woman, and as prepared as anyone could ever be for what was happening to her. Whatever abilities Lucilla had Miranda was sure she wouldn't find her an easy victim.

Even so, despite her confidence, Miranda knew she was passing out – which was when Lucilla would finish what she was doing to her. She knew she had only seconds left in which to act.

Miranda looked inside the car. Daisy was free of Lucilla, but the exhaust fumes would kill her unless Miranda got her out.

As what felt like rough, apelike fingers tore through her head, Miranda pulled the door open, reached inside the car and dragged Daisy out, watching her tumble to the ground. At the same time Lucilla's grasp on her weakened. She was about to return to the child, Miranda knew as she turned and ran towards the motorway, Lucilla still inside her skull. The pain grew worse and she screamed at the agony as if her head were about to explode.

Miranda clenched her teeth against it, aware Lucilla was terrified now. Lucilla hated open spaces. She was petrified of them. In between the bursts of pain Miranda could hear what the girl heard too. Huge wings flapped somewhere overhead. Even though she could see nothing there, she knew Lucilla could. Images, like strands of broken film, flashed through her mind – of something dark and angular with claws like ice-picks, impossibly long. She seemed momentarily to be in another place, a nightmarish world of crimson flames and clouds of ragged, dark grey smoke, all boiling up into a purple sky. Winged creatures flittered across it, battling each other ferociously. Some were killed and torn apart. Others swooped or soared, looking for fresh enemies. One looked down and saw her. Its face, like a horned devil's, was filled with rage as it flapped its wings and dived towards her. And in that instant Miranda knew she had looked into Hell, that somehow Lucilla was part of that place and had escaped from it.

Then, as suddenly as it had started, the vision faded, and Miranda saw she had stepped out onto the motorway and an articulated lorry was heading her way. Without hesitation she ran towards it, determined to let the onrushing vehicle put an end to her and to Lucilla, when the air pushed ahead of it buffeted her towards the hard shoulder, out of its way. In that instant something hard and sharp gripped her shoulders. And for a terrifying second she saw the creature from her vision, its face only inches from her own, dribbling as it clamped its teeth in a seething grin. Then it flung her hard…

7

Travelling with his wife and ten-year old daughter to Luton Airport, Harry Kenyon slammed the brakes of his Toyota. Tyres squealed as the lorry ahead of him jack-knifed across the motorway.

Behind him his daughter screamed. At the same time his wife gave a cry of alarm.

Harry grimaced. Bile burned at the back of his throat as what looked like blood sprayed from the front of the lorry which he somehow miraculously managed to swerve around, heading towards the hard shoulder, too shocked to drive any further. His hands shook as he unfastened his seat belt, fumbling inside his jacket for his mobile phone while cars shot past, skidding to avoid the lorry. A pile up was only seconds away.

"I'll call for an ambulance."

His daughter sobbed.

"It's all right, darling," his wife said to her, though Harry knew it was a lie. A white lie. The kind you told your children when bad things happened.

The girl sobbed again, before she stretched her body in a spasmodic manner and heaved a sigh so deep it made the hair at the back of her father's neck prickle. Twisting around he looked at his daughter as she stared stiffly back at him, and for a moment he was sure she didn't even know who he was – before her eyes shut tight then opened once more and she peered through the window.

"It's all right," the girl said in a voice her father barely recognised. "Everything's all right now."

He looked back and saw his daughter push herself deep into the gap behind his chair and the seat of hers as if she were trying to hide. There was a look of fear in her face.

SWORDS & SORCERIES

TALES OF HEROIC FANTASY

PARALLEL UNIVERSE PUBLICATIONS

Childe Rolande
The Myth and the Legend

Childe Rolande, Hermaphrodite and Freak, is born into the fiercely matriarchal society of Alba at a time when the fabric of the nation is crumbling.

Rolande fulfils all the technical requirements of an ancient Prophesy which promises that one day a 'Redeemer' will arise who will be 'the one and the both', and who will sweep away the age-old tyranny of Alba's female rulers to 'bind the nation together in peace'.

The hopes and dreams of Alba's downtrodden males are centred on this mystical being, whose eyes hold the wisdom of the ages and who can reputedly change into an eagle at will.

Can Rolande live up to their expectations, wrest the antlered throne from the Warlord of the Clans, drive the evil Sorceress, Fergeal from her stronghold in the Dark Tower, and unite the polarised Kingdom?

A seething dark fantasy set in a dystopian Scotland in the far future, where myth and magic are alive once more, *Childe Rolande* is a gritty, no holds barred story of bloodshed and mayhem, of betrayal and brutality.

Optioned to be filmed as a TV mini-series, Samantha Lee is already at work on a sequel.

Available as a paperback and a kindle e-book.

kindle

PARALLEL UNIVERSE PUBLICATIONS

ANTHOLOGIES:

Kitchen Sink Gothic Volumes 1 & 2

Classic Weird Volumes 1 & 2

Things That Go Bump in the Night